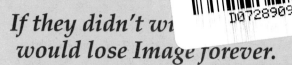

If they didn't win...
would lose Image forever.

Melanie hurried from the office, down the aisle, and into Image's stall. The filly turned to look at her with huge dark eyes. A strand of hay hung from her mouth, and when she saw Melanie, she nickered throatily. "Oh, Image." Melanie put her arms around the filly's silky neck. "I can't believe I almost lost you!"

Pulling back, Melanie stared in wonder at the black filly. Unruffled by the news, Image dropped her head and snatched another bite of hay. "I almost lost you," Melanie whispered, the next words rising in her throat like bile, "to Brad Townsend."

She swallowed, determined never to even think those thoughts again. A month would give her plenty of time to get Image ready for a maiden race at Turfway.

Image will win, Melanie thought. *I'm certain of it.* Then a frown clouded her face as she recalled Mike's terse words: *There is no certainty in racing.*

Placing her cheek against the filly's neck, Melanie closed her eyes, not wanting to acknowledge what *was* certain about Image's first race.

The filly had to win.

Collect all the books in the Thoroughbred series

THOROUGHBRED Super Editions

Ashleigh's Christmas Miracle
Ashleigh's Diary
Ashleigh's Hope
Samantha's Journey

ASHLEIGH'S Thoroughbred Collection

Star of Shadowbrook Farm
The Forgotten Filly
Battlecry Forever!

* coming soon

THOROUGHBRED

RACING IMAGE

CREATED BY
JOANNA CAMPBELL

WRITTEN BY
ALICE LEONHARDT

HarperEntertainment
An Imprint of HarperCollinsPublishers

HarperEntertainment

An Imprint of HarperCollins*Publishers*
10 East 53rd Street, New York, NY 10022-5299

Produced by 17th Street Productions, an Alloy Online, Inc., company

HarperCollins books are available at special quantity discounts for bulk purchases for sales promotions, premiums, or fund-raising. For information please call or write: Special Markets Department, HarperCollins Publishers Inc., 10 East 53rd Street, New York, NY 10022-5299. Telephone: (212) 207-7528. Fax: (212) 207-7222.

ISBN 0-06-106670-2

HarperCollins®, ®, and HarperEntertainment™ are trademarks of HarperCollins Publishers Inc.

Cover art © 2001 by 17th Street Productions, an Alloy Online, Inc., company

First printing: April 2001

Printed in the United States of America

Visit HarperEntertainment on the World Wide Web at
www.harpercollins.com

❖ 10 9 8 7 6 5 4 3 2

"WAKE-UP CALL!" MELANIE GRAHAM CALLED INTO HER cousin Christina Reese's room.

"Go away," Christina mumbled.

It was five-thirty in the morning and pitch black outside. The night before, Melanie and Christina had been up late studying for a history test. Neither of them was ready to get up, but morning came early on a Thoroughbred farm.

And Image was waiting.

Just the thought of Perfect Image made Melanie smile as she headed downstairs to the kitchen. The fractious filly had been at Whitebrook Farm for two weeks. Melanie had given her several days to settle in before resuming working with her. Since then, training had been slow but steady.

1

The first time Melanie had laid eyes on the intelligent, spirited, *spoiled* black filly, she knew Image wouldn't be like any other horse she'd ever worked with. Image had proven her right—many times. Melanie had been stomped, dragged, thrown, and, worst of all, ignored by the opinionated two-year-old.

Image had failed to be manageable enough to train at the track, and her trainer, Vince Jones, had given up. Fortunately, Image's owner, Fredericka Graber, believed in the filly enough to give her a second chance even when Brad Townsend had pressured her to sell Image to him for breeding, saying Image would never make it as a racehorse. Melanie had convinced Fredericka that the filly needed more time in training. Melanie had also convinced Fredericka that she was the only person patient and determined enough to train Image. Granted, things hadn't gone perfectly since then, but now that Image was at Whitebrook, Melanie was confident that she and the filly were on the right track.

Melanie went into the kitchen. A loaf of raisin bread and a container of margarine sat near the toaster. Ashleigh and Mike were already at the barn, checking over each filly and colt before they headed out for their morning works. Melanie popped in two pieces of bread. While they were toasting, she poured two mugs of milk.

Minutes later Christina clomped into the kitchen,

already wearing her paddock boots. Silently Melanie handed her cousin a slice of buttered toast. Melanie ate standing up. The sports section of the newspaper was open on the table, and she read while she chewed.

The previous day a reporter had spent an hour at Whitebrook interviewing Christina and her parents about Christina's horse, Wonder's Star. "Wait until you hear this stupid headline—'Wonder's Star: Fit or Finished?'" Melanie read, her voice rising angrily. "Fit or *finished*? What's this jerk talking about? Star's doing great."

"What do they know?" Christina said with a shrug. "We know Star's coming back, better than ever, right?" Star had been sick for weeks. It had taken all Christina's perseverance, and a trip out west, to get the colt back on his feet. Christina headed to the mud room. "They should write about that crazy Melanie Graham," she continued. "Ever heard of her? She's training this wild horse that everybody else gave up on."

Laughing, Melanie followed her cousin into the mud room, where she stuck her feet into her paddock boots and slipped into her windbreaker. "Wait till Image and I turn up at the track this Christmas and beat all the competition. That'll give them something to write about."

Ten minutes later Melanie was walking down the hill to Image's paddock, a halter and lead shank in her hand. The morning air was so cold it had slapped her awake, but then she saw Image trotting over to the fence to greet her, and a warm rush filled her. The black filly's strides were long and smooth, and she seemed to float over the frosty grass. Her dark eyes sparkled and her tail streamed out behind her.

"Keep her on her toes," Ian McLean, Whitebrook's head trainer, had advised when Image first came to Whitebrook. "If she gets bored, she's going to make trouble."

Melanie knew how much trouble Image could be, so for the past two weeks she had followed the trainer's advice. First she had used Pirate, Image's paddock-mate, to pony Image up and down hills, around the track, and into the woods. Next she'd ridden Image while Kevin McLean, Ian's son and her good friend, ponied them. Each morning they'd varied their ride, saving a trot around the training oval for last, making it special, so that Image would associate the track with fun. In January Image would turn three. By now, most two-year-olds had been in several races, but Image hadn't been ready.

When Melanie reached the gate, Image was dancing on the other side of the fence, tossing her head and whickering deep in her throat. Behind her, Pirate waited quietly. The blind ex-racehorse was used to Image's antics. He was very patient with the high-spirited filly, but when she got too bossy, Pirate didn't hesitate to put her in her place with a well-aimed nip.

Opening the gate, Melanie ran her hand down the filly's silky cheek. Image nuzzled Melanie's neck and snuffled her jacket pockets, looking for a treat. Melanie slipped on the halter, thinking back to the time when even that had been a challenge.

Thank goodness I never gave up, Melanie thought as she opened the gate and led Image out. Eager to get to the barn, the filly pranced sideways. Pirate followed behind, using his senses of smell and hearing to find his way up the hill. Since Image hated to be cooped up in a stall, Melanie had decided to keep her turned out night and day. Image and Pirate had a run-in shed for bad weather, and Ian had set aside a large foaling stall for the filly for days when it turned snowy or icy. So far, it had been a perfect strategy. Image glowed with health.

When they reached the barn, Melanie turned Image around and hooked her up to crossties. The filly flung her head up and whinnied, but she calmed down when she saw Pirate duck into the first stall, which was ready for him, the feed bucket full of grain.

Melanie shut Pirate's stall door, then started unbuckling Image's blanket. In the aisle behind them, Jonnie and Dani were grooming two other youngsters in crossties. Image flung her head from side to side, trying to look at them. When one of them whinnied, she squealed and pawed the aisle in reply.

Melanie rolled her eyes. "You are so much trouble," she told Image as she slid her blanket off.

"Morning," someone said in a sleepy voice. Melanie turned to see Kevin walking down the aisle toward her, a grooming box in his hand.

"Hey, you old witch," he said affectionately, rubbing Image's nose. Kevin was one of the few guys the filly liked. "Ready for me and Pirate to beat you and Mel?" Grinning, Kevin looked over at Melanie.

She snorted. "Is that a challenge, McLean?"

Kevin chuckled. "I knew you couldn't resist."

"I never miss a chance to beat you. And Image is ready." When Kevin left to groom Pirate, Melanie stepped back and ran her gaze admiringly over the filly. Image had well-defined muscles, a deep chest, and high, powerful haunches. Her shoulders were sloped just right, and her long legs had flat knees and massive cannon bones.

Perfect conformation for a champion, Melanie thought as she plucked a brush from the grooming box. Since she'd been at Whitebrook, Image had gained some weight, and hours of grooming had turned her coat from scruffy to silky. She was in top condition.

By the time she'd groomed and tacked up the filly, Christina and Star were coming in from their morning workout. Christina was leading Star, and Melanie could tell from the grin on her cousin's face that their workout had been a good one.

When they walked past, Image spun in a circle and half dragged Melanie down the aisle after the chestnut colt.

"I guess she has good taste!" Christina teased.

"Whoa!" Melanie said, digging in her heels and forcing Image to halt. The filly's manners were terrible. "You're getting a double workout this morning!" she growled. "I want to get you good and tired."

She heard Kevin laugh from Pirate's stall. "Correction. *You* will be good and tired." He led Pirate out, and Image danced happily at the sight of her paddock-mate, almost tromping on Melanie's toes.

When she led Image outside to mount, Jonnie boosted her up into the saddle before Image could even think about bolting. Swinging her head around, Image tried to bite the stable hand's arm, but Jonnie stuck out his elbow and caught her square on her nose instead. Startled, Image threw back her head, an indignant look in her expressive eyes.

Melanie bit back a smile. Everybody was working hard to teach Image manners, but it wasn't easy. Kevin steered Pirate beside them. "Warm-up trot in the pasture?" he asked.

Melanie nodded as she snapped her helmet strap. "Definitely."

The foursome headed for one of the rolling pastures behind Whitebrook's broodmare barn. As they passed the barn, Joe Kisner led out two mares, one on either side of him, a lead line in each hand. The mares' bellies were huge, and they moved slowly down the path to the pasture. Joe nodded hello. When he came alongside with the mares, Image pinned her ears threateningly and snaked her head toward them. Melanie dug her heel in the filly's left side and tightened her right rein, signaling her to move away. Reluctantly Image obeyed, but not without a defiant swish of her tail, as if trying to have the last word.

"Oh, Kevin, what if she never gets used to other horses?" Melanie said to her friend, who was plodding quietly beside them on Pirate. "What if she freaks out when she's out on the track with a whole field of horses?"

Kevin shrugged. "Then you've got a problem. But I don't think it's one you can't handle in training. She's fine with Pirate, and she seems to like Star. Let's see how cantering with Pirate goes today. Maybe if she does well, you can try her with Star tomorrow."

"Good plan," Melanie replied. "I'll talk to Chris and Ashleigh about it when we get back."

Once inside the pasture, the horses broke into a trot. Image jigged sideways, her back humped as if she wanted to buck. Melanie clamped her legs against the filly's sides, forcing her to extend her stride and move forward. After a few hills the filly's back relaxed, and her trot felt so strong and rhythmic that Melanie smiled at the sheer pleasure of riding the horse she loved so much.

When Image finally started blowing, they slowed to a walk. Pirate's neck was dark with sweat, but the powerful six-year-old was well conditioned and kept up easily with the two-year-old.

Melanie looked over at the training oval. It was empty. "Ready?"

Kevin nodded, and they made their way from the pasture to the gap in the railing of Whitebrook's practice track. Every morning Joe raked the track smooth. Now the sandy brown footing was already bumpy and uneven from the morning works. Image minced across the track, her neck arched, as if she were heading for Keeneland's starting gate. Melanie's heart beat faster.

Melanie and Image followed Kevin and Pirate clockwise on the outside rail to the three-eighths pole. Then they cut across to the inside rail. When they began to trot counterclockwise, Melanie's stomach twisted in a knot. Image's behavior on the track had ranged from crazy to outright dangerous. What if she bolted and Melanie lost control?

"It'll be okay," Kevin called to her.

He must see how nervous I am, Melanie thought. She took a few deep breaths and forced herself to think positively. Image's trot was calm, and her ears were pricked. When Kevin glanced at Melanie once more, she nodded, signaling that she was ready.

Kevin clucked and asked Pirate for a canter. The black gelding had a ground-covering stride and instantly moved ahead. Image's ears flicked, and she stuck her nose in the air, eager for a race. Melanie felt the filly's muscles tense. She leaned forward and told the horse to canter.

Image needed no further encouragement. With two bounding leaps, she caught up with Pirate, tossed her head haughtily, and surged ahead. Melanie kept her seat up off the young horse's back, her weight on her heels, rocking to the motion of Image's rhythmic stride. The filly was eager yet controlled, and when Melanie tightened her fingers on the outside rein, Image veered to the left. Then she jiggled the left rein, and Image moved to the rail.

Melanie grinned. Image was listening to her. The weeks of training had paid off.

Melanie touched her heels to Image's sides. The filly's stride lengthened, and her hooves rose and fell, pounding the soft earth.

When they reached the finish line, Melanie stood in her stirrups and gave gentle half-halts on the reins. Image tossed her head, then settled into a trot. She jogged the filly another furlong, then dropped down to a walk. Leaning forward, Melanie hugged Image around her sweat-darkened neck.

Kevin jogged up on Pirate. "I think you've got yourself a racehorse!" he panted.

"You mean *Fredericka's* got a racehorse," Melanie corrected, suddenly noticing Image's owner standing by the exit gate. Taking the reins in one hand, she raised the other in a wave of hello. "I wonder what she's doing here this early."

Melanie had spent many weeks at Tall Oaks, Fredericka's farm, working with Image, and she had gotten to know Fredericka well. The older woman was a widow, and Image had been born the same month Fredericka's husband, Charles, had died. Fredericka had poured all her love into the filly, spoiling her rotten, which was one of the reasons Image was so difficult.

Melanie smiled, glad that Fredericka had picked this morning to stop by and see Image's workout. But when she rode closer, her smile faded. Fredericka's face was pale and drawn. Something was wrong.

"Hi, Fredericka," Melanie said cheerfully, trying not to sound anxious. "Is everything all right?"

Fredericka shook her head and brushed stray tendrils of gray hair away from her face. "No, I'm sorry to say everything's not all right, Melanie."

Melanie dismounted and led Image through the gap. The filly pressed her muzzle against Fredericka's outstretched hand. "Hello, my princess," Fredericka crooned, her voice faltering. Melanie saw tears glimmer in the older woman's eyes, and she knew that whatever was bothering Fredericka had to do with Image.

"Fredericka, tell me what's wrong," Melanie said, the words catching in her throat.

"Everything," Fredericka sighed as she stroked Image's neck. "You know that when Alexis quit so abruptly two weeks ago, she left me with financial problems. Well, I hired an accountant to go over the farm's account books."

Melanie swallowed hard. Alexis Huffman had been the manager of Tall Oaks. Fredericka had trusted her completely, relying on Alexis's advice for everything, including buying and selling new horses. Unfortunately, Alexis had taken advantage of Fredericka's trust. She'd steered the older woman into buying wildly expensive horses as well as selling some of the farm's valuable yearlings. Later it was discovered that Alexis was recommending purchases and sales based on how much commission she'd earn, not whether the transactions made sense for Tall Oaks.

"Wh-what did the accountant say?" Melanie stammered.

"He said I was hugely in debt and that if I didn't sell off some of my horses, the farm would go bankrupt. He recommended that I keep Gratis, because he's been winning enough money to pay his way, and Khan, since I already have over twenty mares booked to breed to him next year. But he said I have to sell any horse who isn't actively making money. . . ." Her voice trailed off. Pulling a tissue from her pocket, she pressed it to the corners of her eyes.

Melanie swallowed hard. "Oh, Fredericka, I'm so sorry," she whispered, a sob catching in her throat.

"No, Melanie. *I'm* so sorry." Fredericka reached for Melanie's hand and held on tightly. "You've been doing such a good job training Image. I had such high hopes, and now . . ."

Silently the two turned their eyes toward Image. Melanie knew what Fredericka meant. Image was only costing her money.

She would have to be sold.

2

"HEY, WHAT'S WITH THE GLOOMY FACES?" KEVIN ASKED AS he led Pirate through the gap. "Image looked awesome out there. I figured you two were planning her first race."

"Nope, it looks like some stranger's going to be planning Image's first race," Melanie said, using the sleeve of her windbreaker to wipe away her tears. Turning, she laid her cheek against the filly's damp neck and squeezed her eyelids shut. Her heart felt as if it had broken in two.

Kevin stopped so fast that Pirate bumped into him. "What are you talking about?"

Melanie looked at Fredericka, but the older woman shook her head, unable to talk.

"Is it all right if I tell Kevin?" Melanie asked her.

14

When Fredericka nodded, Melanie took a ragged breath, then filled Kevin in as they led the horses slowly toward the barn.

"But Image *will* pay her way," Kevin said when Melanie had finished talking. "As soon as she gets on the track."

"Yes, but the bank won't wait," Fredericka said. "If I don't pay my debts, I'm going to lose Tall Oaks. I'm sorry," she apologized again, touching Melanie's shoulder.

"It's not your fault. If anyone is to blame, it's Alexis," Melanie told her.

Fredericka's smile was resigned. "What Alexis did was morally wrong but not legally wrong. I should never have allowed her to manipulate me. I should have questioned her advice."

"That's tough," Kevin said, shaking his head.

"Well," Melanie declared, "I'm not giving up yet." Her anger at Alexis had suddenly energized her. "Image and I haven't come this far for her to be sold to some thickheaded trainer like Vince, who will run her too soon, or, worse, to Brad, who will turn her into a sway-backed broodmare."

Brad Townsend, owner of Townsend Acres, knew Image had good bloodlines, and he had been pressuring Fredericka to sell the filly to him to keep as a broodmare. But Fredericka had turned him down, as convinced as Melanie that Image still had a chance on the track. Now all that was about to change.

Dropping her chin, Fredericka looked down at her hands, which were clenched tightly.

Melanie let out a gasp. "You didn't sell Image to Brad already, did you?"

Just then Ashleigh Griffen came over. "Hello, Fredericka," she greeted the older woman warmly before turning to flash Melanie and Kevin a stern look. "Why aren't you two walking your mounts? They're going to stiffen up or catch a cold."

Numb with shock, Melanie barely heard her aunt. "Fredericka? Did you sell Image already?" she repeated.

"No, not yet," Fredericka said in a low voice.

Ashleigh's brows shot up as she looked from Melanie to Fredericka. "Have I missed something?"

"Something major," Kevin answered glumly.

"Well, by the looks on everybody's faces, whatever this 'something' is, it needs discussing," Ashleigh said in a no-nonsense voice. "But not until these horses are cooled off. Fredericka, why don't you go wait in the office? I'll get you some coffee." She put her arm around Fredericka and steered her toward the barn. "Melanie," she called over her shoulder, "when you're through with Image, meet us in the office, and we'll talk about what's going on."

Melanie nodded. Turning, she laid her palm against the filly's warm cheek. Image gazed at her so trustingly that Melanie had to choke back a sob.

Kevin touched her shoulder. "Anything I can do?"

She shook her head, tears blurring her eyes. "I was supposed to exercise Raven this morning. Will you tell Cindy I can't?"

Kevin squeezed her shoulder and led Pirate off to the barn. Melanie stood frozen next to Image. Impatiently the filly shoved Melanie with her nose, and Melanie forced a smile through her tears. "I know. Time to get this saddle off," she said. Lifting the blanket, she loosened the girth. Her movements were automatic, her mind numb.

Dani walked over, a halter and lead shank hanging from her shoulder. "Would you like me to cool her off for you?" she asked.

Melanie shook her head. "Thanks, Dani. I'll do it." Sighing, she led Image into the barn and started untacking her. Jonnie was bathing a colt in the wash stall, and Dani came by leading Raven down the aisle. Both grooms gave Melanie sidelong glances, but neither said anything. Melanie knew they had heard—news traveled fast around the farm.

Twenty minutes later Image was bathed and cool. Melanie had covered her with two woolen coolers and stuck her in the empty stall. "I'll be back," she told the filly. "Right now Fredericka and I have something important to talk about—you."

Lingering for a moment, Melanie leaned against

17

the stall wall and watched Image munch on a flake of sweet hay. Her heart swelled with pride as she thought how far the filly had come in the past few weeks. What would happen when Image left Whitebrook? Would she ever see her again?

Suddenly Melanie caught herself. Why was she acting as if Image were already sold? Why was she giving up? She'd fought for Image before. She could do it again.

She left the stall, her stride determined as she headed down the aisle to the office. Yanking open the door, she stepped inside, ready to do anything she could for Image.

Ashleigh and Fredericka turned in their chairs and looked at her. Both held steaming mugs in their hands. Mike Reese, Ashleigh's husband, was propped against the desk, his arms folded against his chest.

"Fredericka, I know you and Tall Oaks are in trouble," Melanie said before she lost her nerve. "But I'll die if you sell Image and I never get to see her again. I mean, I won't die—" Melanie stopped. If she was going to convince Fredericka not to sell Image, she had to make sense. "What I mean is, Image should be ready to race by the end of the month. If there's any way you can give her a chance, I think she *will* pay her own way, and soon."

Fredericka glanced down at her mug as if afraid to meet Melanie's gaze.

"I would love to give Image the time she needs," Fredericka said, her voice so soft Melanie had to strain to hear her. "But I can't afford to. The bank isn't interested in how much I care about my horses. They're only interested in their money."

"Then let *me* buy Image!" Melanie exclaimed. She knew how ridiculous it sounded. But she couldn't give up. "I've saved a few thousand dollars from racing. It could be a down payment. I can quit school and start jockeying full time," she added, her voice rising. "And when Image starts winning, I'll pay you back with purse money."

"Oh, Melanie." Reaching out, Fredericka took her hand.

"Melanie, I know you're upset, but you're not being realistic," Mike broke in. "Ashleigh and I aren't going to let you quit school. Besides, you know how uncertain racing is. Image could be the next Derby winner, or she could break down in her first race."

"But I can't give up," Melanie said desperately. "I *can't*."

"I understand, Melanie," Fredericka said kindly. "But I'm in a bind. As I was telling your aunt and uncle, Brad has offered to help me out by paying a generous amount for several of my broodmares and yearlings, including Image's dam, Townsend Mistress."

Right, like he really wants to help you out, Melanie wanted to say.

"He's always wanted to get his hands on Image's mother," Ashleigh said, obviously having the same thought.

"Yes, but it's not just Mistress he wants." Fredericka exhaled wearily. "He's insisting that Image be part of the package."

Melanie's heart sank. No matter how hard she worked or what she offered, she could never beat Brad Townsend. "Then it's a done deal," she said flatly.

"Not quite." Mike straightened. "Before you came in, we were discussing some options with Fredericka."

"Options?" Melanie felt a flutter of hope.

"We told Fredericka that Image is welcome to stay the rest of the month at Whitebrook—for free."

"You'd do that?" Melanie asked, astonished.

Ashleigh laughed. "Mel, you're like a daughter to us. And we know how much Image means to you. As long as you keep training and caring for her, it should work out. But it's still up to Fredericka. Brad's offer *is* very generous, and it sounds like it will completely solve the farm's financial problems."

Melanie turned her hopeful gaze on Fredericka, who was rubbing the bridge of her nose. Melanie felt sorry for the older woman. Fredericka loved Image, too. She loved all her horses. And because of Alexis, she could lose everything.

Stooping next to Fredericka's chair, Melanie squeezed the older woman's hand. "Ashleigh's right. I'll understand if you choose Brad's offer. Tall Oaks is your home, and you have to do what you can to save it. Besides, Brad will probably let me come visit Image—every leap year," she added, trying to be funny, but her voice cracked.

Fredericka patted Melanie's hand. "Oh, Melanie. Thank you for understanding, but you know what? I was raised as a proper Southern lady, and it would be rude of me to refuse your aunt and uncle's most generous offer to keep Image at Whitebrook. I'll just have to tell Brad a little white lie. I'll tell him the bank has frozen my assets and won't let me sell the horses until the beginning of the new year."

"You mean—?"

"You can have Image until the end of December," Fredericka said, breaking into a smile. "Do you think you can make a racehorse out of her by then?"

"Yes! Yes! Yes!" Melanie jumped up. "Image and I won't let you down. I promise."

"Ahem." Mike cleared his throat loudly. "I hate to be the one to mention this, but Fredericka, you owe the bank money. If you delay the sale to Brad, how are you going to pay them?"

A steely glint came into Fredericka's eyes. "Melanie's determination made me realize that I shouldn't give up so easily, either." She tipped her chin. "I know many of the bank's directors, and it's time I reminded them that my family has been banking with their company for generations. I think that should command a little respect."

"What if Brad doesn't want to wait until the new year?" Mike continued. "What if he withdraws his offer?"

"Then it's Brad's loss," Fredericka said simply. "Tall Oaks may not be a large farm, but it has a sterling reputation. Charles and I have sold horses to many satisfied owners and trainers. I'll be delighted to sell my animals to someone who truly appreciates fine stock."

"That's the spirit," Ashleigh said, and she and Melanie began clapping.

"What's all the excitement about?" The door opened, and Cindy McLean, Ian's adopted daughter, came into the office. The young jockey had recently had surgery on her rotator cuff, and her arm was in a sling to keep her shoulder immobile.

"We're excited that Brad won't get his hands on Image," Melanie said.

For a second Cindy looked horrified. "Don't tell me you were thinking of selling Image to that piranha!" she said to Fredericka. "Has anyone ever told Mrs. Graber the story of how Brad and Lavinia ruined Townsend Princess?"

"That was long ago," Fredericka said.

Cindy opened her mouth as if to disagree, but Ashleigh gave her a look of warning.

"The Grabers have been friends with the Townsends for years," Ashleigh said diplomatically.

"Brad has been a great help since Alexis left," Fredericka said. "He's going to help me get good prices for the horses I need to sell." She sighed. "And I do need to sell some stock. Elizabeth is trying to keep up with the barn work, but I'm afraid it's too much for one person. I've been so distraught, I haven't been any help at all. Tomorrow Gratis is coming back to the farm to recover from a stone bruise." She threw her hands in the air. "I don't know what to do."

"You need to hire someone," Mike said. "Especially if you're keeping Khan. Breeding season will be here before you know it, and you'll definitely need help with that."

"Yes, but my experience with Alexis left me sort of gun-shy," Fredericka admitted. "She came with wonderful recommendations, and look what happened. How can I trust anyone again?"

"I can come over some afternoons," Melanie volunteered. "It's the least I can do."

"That's fine, dear, but don't take time away from my princess. She comes first."

"I can help, too," Cindy chimed in. "Especially with Gratis. I have plenty of experience with stone bruises."

Ashleigh raised one brow. "Are you sure? What about your shoulder?"

"Positive," Cindy answered brusquely. "My shoulder is *fine*."

23

Melanie knew that Cindy's shoulder wasn't fine, but she also knew how much Cindy wanted to get back to riding again. For the past ten years Cindy had been a prize-winning jockey, traveling and racing all over the United States and overseas. But she had suffered a shoulder injury some years before, and this summer it had gotten so bad that Cindy had been forced to take time off and have surgery. She hated not being able to ride, and she was restless and ornery.

"I would love help from someone with your expertise," Fredericka told Cindy. "I'm afraid Alexis left things in quite a muddle."

"Fredericka, thanks again for believing in me—and Image," Melanie said. "Now I'd better go tell Image the great news!"

Melanie hurried from the office, down the aisle, and into Image's stall. The filly turned to look at her with huge dark eyes. A strand of hay hung from her mouth, and when she saw Melanie, she nickered throatily. "Oh, Image." Melanie put her arms around the filly's silky neck. "I can't believe I almost lost you!"

Pulling back, Melanie stared in wonder at the black filly. Unruffled by the news, Image dropped her head and snatched another bite of hay. "I almost lost you," Melanie whispered, the next words rising in her throat like bile, "to Brad Townsend."

She swallowed, determined never to even think those thoughts again. A month would give her plenty of time to get Image ready for a maiden race at Turf-way.

Image will win, Melanie thought. *I'm certain of it.* Then a frown clouded her face as she recalled Mike's terse words: *There is no certainty in racing.*

Placing her cheek against the filly's neck, Melanie closed her eyes, not wanting to acknowledge what *was* certain about Image's first race.

The filly had to win.

3

IMAGE STARED AT THE STARTING GATE, EYES ROLLING, EARS laid back against her head. Melanie sat quietly in the saddle. Ian stood at Image's head, the lead shank held lightly in one hand. With his other hand he stroked her neck.

"Nothing to be scared of," he told the filly, but Image danced backward as if she didn't believe him.

"She's just being stubborn, Ian," Melanie said through clenched teeth. It was Thursday morning. They'd been standing by the gate for half an hour, trying to coax Image closer. It was cold and gray, and the frosty wind had numbed Melanie's ears and fingers. Ian had a knit cap pulled over his head, and his cheeks were red. Even Image had her tail tucked against the brisk wind.

"She doesn't have a scared bone in her body," Melanie continued. "She's just feeling good and wants an excuse to buck me off."

Ian chuckled. It was two days after Fredericka's visit. Melanie, Ashleigh, and Ian had come up with a schedule for Image's training. If the filly was going to race at the end of the month, she had to be ready. Breaking clean from a starting gate was one of the most important skills Image had to master before she would be allowed to race.

"Calm down," Ian said. "Remember, when a horse is spooky, you want to be like a lump of clay—stuck tight to the saddle, but not interfering."

"I know," Melanie grumbled, willing herself to relax.

Ian had opened both doors in the stall of the starting gate. All Image had to do that morning was walk through. At Whitebrook, the yearlings were routinely led in and out of the stalls. By the time they were two, they were completely unfazed by the metal contraption. But this was Image's first experience with the starting gate, and Melanie could tell she wanted nothing to do with it.

"Walk on," Melanie said confidently. But the black filly planted her feet firmly and refused to budge. "You're just being pigheaded, mulish, and ornery," Melanie scolded. Image only flicked her ears in response.

For the next fifteen minutes Melanie and Ian crooned and cajoled, but the filly wouldn't budge.

Blowing out her breath, Melanie resisted the urge to kick the stubborn horse forward. But Image had to do it on her own, or for the rest of her racing days someone would have to force her in.

"Let's look on the bright side," Melanie finally said to Ian. "If we stand here all day, I'll be late for my chemistry quiz. That is, if I don't freeze first."

"And I won't have to listen to Cindy grumble about not being able to do anything on account of her shoulder," Ian said.

"She's really cranky, isn't she?" Melanie said.

Ian nodded. "Even Beth is frustrated. Nothing we do seems to help. The only thing that's going to lift her spirits is for the doctor to tell her she can ride again."

What if she can't? Melanie wanted to ask, but she figured Ian didn't want to even think about the possibility.

Suddenly Image moved forward, yanking the lead from Ian's grasp, and walked through the starting gate stall to the other side. Relieved, Melanie leaned forward and stretched out her hand to feed the filly a carrot.

"Don't tell me we wore her out," she said to Ian when he came up to retrieve the dangling lead.

He laughed. "Nope. She was just biding her time. She needed to make up her own mind and do it on her terms."

Melanie straightened in the saddle. "Should we take her through it again?"

Ian shook his head. "She'd feel insulted. She honored us by doing it once. Let's quit on a good note and do it again tomorrow."

"Good idea," Melanie said. She had already worked Image with Kevin and Pirate, and the filly had earned her breakfast. She headed back to the barn and saw Cindy walking Fast Gun, a high-strung colt who'd been gelded because he'd gotten too dangerous to handle.

"Hey, Cindy," Melanie said as she dismounted. "Want to go over to Fredericka's with me when I get back from school?"

Cindy shrugged. "I guess," she said. Melanie wondered if Cindy had changed her mind or if she wasn't all that enthusiastic about helping out at Tall Oaks.

"You don't have to," Melanie said.

"Hey, what else do I have to do?" Cindy answered, as if she didn't care one way or the other. Turning, she led Fast Gun in the other direction.

Well, excuse me for asking, Melanie wanted to say. She and Christina had tried to be sensitive to Cindy's moods, since they both knew how devastated they would be if they had to quit riding. But Cindy's moodiness was easy to mistake for meanness.

"Kind of like you when you don't get your way," Melanie teased when the filly nipped her on the arm. She loosened the girth, her eyes following Cindy, who was leading the colt in the grassy area in front of the barn.

Cindy acted as if she thought taking care of horses was beneath her. Most jockeys had that attitude. But as far as Melanie was concerned, taking care of Image was a pleasure and a privilege, and one day Image was going to surprise everyone.

"Elizabeth?" Melanie called that afternoon as she and Cindy walked down the dark aisle of the barn at Tall Oaks. "Are you here?"

"Doesn't look like it." Cindy had her arms crossed in front of her chest. "Or smell like it," she added, wrinkling her nose.

Melanie knew what she meant. The barn had the distinct odor of sour urine, as if the stalls hadn't been cleaned in days.

Melanie thought back to the first time she'd visited Tall Oaks. The barn had been spotless. Stopping in front of a stall, Melanie peered in. A horse in a manure-stained blanket peered back at her.

"I wonder how long it's been since these guys were turned out," Cindy commented.

"At least they've been fed and watered," Melanie said, noting that the hay nets and water buckets were full. "Elizabeth's been taking classes at Kentucky State, so it's probably all she's been able to keep up with. I'll say one thing for Alexis—she took good care of the horses," she added reluctantly.

"I'll say." There was a note of admiration in Cindy's voice. "Fredericka has some gorgeous animals."

Melanie walked down to where Cindy was standing. She'd opened the stall door and was patting a coppery bay colt.

"That's Court Jester," Melanie said. "He'll be a two-year-old next year. Alexis convinced Fredericka to buy him right before she quit. Fredericka calls him her 'million-dollar baby.' If she really paid that much for him, Alexis probably made a hundred thousand dollars in commission."

Cindy whistled. "I wish I'd met Alexis. I'd have given her a piece of my mind."

A throaty bellow came from the stallion wing. "That's either Khan or Gratis," Melanie said as they walked down the aisle. "When I talked to Elizabeth earlier, she said Vince had vanned Gratis over here yesterday. She also said Vince was *not* happy about Gratis coming back to Tall Oaks, since there was no farm manager. But I guess Fredericka can't afford to keep him at the track if he's not racing."

Cindy shook her head in dismay. "Thoroughbred racing's an expensive business to be in when you're winning. It's a killer if you're not. I've seen plenty of owners and trainers go bust in my time."

They stopped in front of Gratis's stall. The stunning colt was a dark bay with a white blaze and two white stockings. Gratis was Fredericka's most successful racehorse.

"Chris said she'd help you with him," Melanie said. Christina was one of the few jockeys who'd raced Gratis.

Cindy shot Melanie a sharp look, "Don't take this wrong, but I don't need any tips from Christina."

"O-o-okay." Melanie stepped back, and Cindy opened the stall door. Pinning his ears, Gratis stood his ground. So did Cindy. For what seemed like forever, the two stared at each other. Then Gratis looked away, a wary expression on his face, and Melanie knew that Cindy had won the first round.

Outside the barn, a motor roared to life, then coughed and died. "That sounds like the tractor," Melanie said. "Why don't you check out the other horses and see if they're okay? I'll ask Elizabeth what she wants us to do first."

Cindy went down the aisle, and Melanie headed out the side double doors. Elizabeth Wilson was standing next to the tractor, a wrench in one hand. Grease streaked her face, and when she looked over at Melanie, there were tears in her eyes.

"Hey, what's wrong?" Melanie asked. Elizabeth was in her early twenties. She'd been working for Fredericka for a year and did a great job, but Melanie knew there was no way she could handle all the responsibilities of the farm by herself.

"Everything," she said. "I can't get the tractor to work, and without the tractor I can't pull the manure spreader. Yesterday I used a wheelbarrow, and it took me all day."

"Where's Drew?"

"He quit last week. Not that I blame him. Fredericka keeps forgetting to pay us, and . . ." She bit her lower lip, and a tear rolled down her cheek. "I'll stay whether I get paid or not—I mean, I couldn't stand it if the horses weren't taken care of—but I'm doing such a lousy job, I might as well quit, too. I just can't keep up, Melanie. And Fredericka . . ." She sighed.

"Doesn't have a clue?" Melanie guessed.

Elizabeth nodded. "She's such a dear lady, but I swear she thinks the horses feed themselves." Wiping her eyes, Elizabeth giggled with exhaustion.

"We'll help. Cindy came with me."

"Cindy?"

"Ian's daughter. She's a jockey, but she had her shoulder operated on, so she can't ride. Right now she's one-handed, but she really knows horses."

"Believe me, I'll take any help I can get," Elizabeth said. She turned back to the tractor.

"Did you kick it?" Melanie asked, and the two started laughing. Just then Cindy came out. "Fredericka's stallion looks like he's about to break down his stall door," she said after introducing herself. "When's the last time he was turned out?"

33

"Khan? He's still here?" Elizabeth joked, but her voice had an edge to it. "Actually, I'm surprised Brad Townsend hasn't bought him yet. He's been here every day, circling the barn like a vulture, waiting for Fredericka to decide which horses she's selling."

"Hey, are you guys having a party out here?"

Melanie swung around as Parker and Christina came out of the barn. They were dressed in sweatshirts and old jeans.

"What are you two doing here?" Melanie asked. "Parker, I thought you were riding at Whisperwood this afternoon."

Parker Townsend, Christina's boyfriend, kept his horse, Foxy, at Whisperwood, Samantha and Tor Nelson's farm. He was training for a spot on the Olympic three-day-event team and rode for several hours every day after his morning classes at the University of Kentucky.

"We thought you guys might need some help," Christina said. "And I wanted to see how Gratis is doing. What're you guys doing out here?" She pointed behind her. "The barn is that way," she joked.

"We're talking about what a vulture Brad Townsend is," Elizabeth said.

"That reminds me. Elizabeth, have you ever met Parker Townsend, Brad's son?" Melanie asked, a gleam in her eye.

Elizabeth's face turned scarlet, and she slapped a

hand over her mouth. "Oh, gosh. I had no idea. Me and my big mouth. I'm so sorry, Parker. I didn't mean to say anything bad about your father."

"Don't worry about it," Parker said, laughing. "It would be hard to say anything *good* about my father."

"Okay, enough chatter. We need to get to work," Cindy said impatiently. "Hand me that wrench, Elizabeth, and let's get this tractor running."

"Chris, why don't you and Parker help me turn out the horses?" Melanie said as the three headed back into the barn. "I can tell you which paddocks they go in. And then we can get started on the stalls."

"Sounds like a plan," Parker said. Melanie pointed out the yearling fillies, who would be turned out together, and the three kids split up, each heading to a different stall. Grabbing a lead line, Melanie walked down the aisle to get Crystal, whose stall was by the barn entrance. She was about to open the filly's door when she heard the sound of tires crunching on gravel. She peered outside, drawing back when she spotted Brad Townsend's car.

What is he doing here? she fumed. Then she remembered Elizabeth's crack about Brad circling the barn like a vulture.

Hurrying, Melanie slid the latch on Crystal's door and ducked inside the stall. "Hey, girl," she whispered to the gray filly, who gave her a curious look. Melanie patted her, then moved around to the yearling's far

35

side. She did *not* want to see Brad Townsend. Brad had been furious when Fredericka decided to send Image to Whitebrook instead of selling the filly to him. Melanie hadn't talked to Brad since then, and she didn't want to now.

". . . some great buys," Melanie heard Brad say to someone as he approached the barn. *Who is he with?* Melanie wondered.

"Take this filly, for instance." Brad sounded so close that Melanie knew he had to be talking about Crystal. The filly moved toward the stall door, exposing Melanie. She dove for a shadowy corner, underneath the water bucket, praying he hadn't heard her. If Brad didn't come into the stall, he wouldn't be able to see her.

"She's got quality written all over her," Brad said in a smooth voice. "Her sire's Key to the Mint. Her dam's Wayward, by Independence. You can't ask for better bloodlines. Mrs. Graber paid over five hundred thousand dollars for her. But since she's desperate to sell and wants the filly to go to a good home, I could probably convince her to part with her for four."

Four! Melanie's eyes widened. Fredericka would lose over a hundred thousand dollars!

"Trust me," Brad added in a low voice. "I can get you a good deal."

Melanie grimaced in disgust and clenched her hands into fists. She wanted to jump up and tell Brad she'd heard everything he'd said, but she felt foolish hiding from him in the first place.

Just then Melanie heard Parker yell, "Dad? What are you doing here?"

"Hey, Parker. I wondered the same thing when I saw your truck outside. Son, I'd like you to meet Mr. and Mrs. Somers. We're training their colt, Miracle Boy. Perhaps you remember him. Won an allowance race last week." Brad's voice was charming and smooth. Melanie couldn't believe what a fake he was.

Melanie heard the murmur of several hellos, and then Brad went on to tell Parker that the Somerses were looking for several new horses. "I told them that Fredericka had some nice ones for sale."

And he's promising they'll be cheap, Melanie thought sarcastically.

"Yeah, she does have some nice horses," Parker said. "Christina and I were just commenting on it. We're helping Melanie turn them out and muck stalls."

"Melanie?"

Melanie bit back a laugh when she heard the change in Brad's voice. Brad wanted Image, and so far Melanie had been his biggest obstacle to buying the filly.

"Yeah. She's helping Fredericka out," Parker said. "I guess when Alexis, her farm manager, quit, she didn't hire anyone else."

"Oh, right. Well, we'll come back another time, then. Perhaps when Fredericka's here."

And I'm not, Melanie added to herself.

Everybody said polite good-byes. Melanie listened for the car to drive away, then stood up. Parker was staring at her through the bars of the stall. Startled, Melanie screamed.

Parker burst out laughing. "I wondered how long you were going to stay hunkered down in the manure."

She clutched her heart. "You scared me to death, Parker Townsend! Did you know I was here the whole time you were talking to your dad?"

"Sure. I saw you go in." He shook his head, chuckling. "I knew the last person you wanted to see was my father, but I didn't think you'd hide."

Reaching up, Melanie snapped the lead line onto Crystal's halter ring. "I'm glad I did. You should have heard what your father was saying to those people before he bumped into you."

"Oh?" Parker looked curiously at her as he opened the stall door.

"I'll fill you in later. We'd better hurry and get these stalls done."

It took the five of them over two hours to muck out the stalls, bed them with fresh straw, bring in the horses, and feed them. When they finally finished, it was dark outside. Exhausted, they met in the tack room, where Elizabeth treated them to sodas she had stashed in the small refrigerator.

38

"Whew," Melanie said as she sat down on a tack box. "We sure do smell nasty."

"But the stalls smell sweet," Christina said, sitting beside her.

Cindy plopped down on a camp chair. "I'm glad I don't have a hot date."

"Me too," Parker said, grinning at Christina.

"Well, I can't thank you guys enough," Elizabeth said. Sitting on the floor, she leaned her head back against the wall. She looked drained but relaxed. "Now I just have to get Fredericka to hire someone before the stalls need cleaning again. Like, tomorrow."

"Tell her you'll place the ad and do the interviewing," Cindy suggested.

"Me?" Elizabeth shook her head emphatically. "No way. I can barely make it through an interview myself without getting so nervous that I feel sick."

"Why don't you help her do it?" Melanie said to Cindy.

Cindy hesitated, and Melanie figured she was going to say no.

"Okay," Cindy said, surprising everyone. "Let's get started first thing in the morning."

Cindy really did care about horses, Melanie realized. Maybe it was just people she had problems dealing with.

"Thank you!" Elizabeth said gratefully.

"That's settled," Parker said. "So, Melanie, what

were you going to tell me about my father?"

Instantly four pairs of eyes swung toward Melanie.

Melanie told them what she'd overheard. When she was finished, Christina's mouth fell open and Elizabeth groaned, but Melanie could tell that Cindy and Parker weren't surprised.

Parker raised his soda can in a toast. "That's my dad."

"The horse world is full of owners and trainers like him," Cindy said. "That's one thing I don't miss about the racetrack."

"What are we going to do?" Elizabeth asked. "I can't stand to see Fredericka getting ripped off again."

"I have another idea," Melanie said. "Cindy, maybe you can help Fredericka determine the current value of the horses she's selling."

"I can do that," Cindy said, sounding interested.

"All right!" Melanie said. As she finished her soda she couldn't help smiling.

If Cindy helped Fredericka price her horses, Fredericka might not be so eager to accept Brad's offers. She might decide not to sell any of her horses to Brad.

Then Melanie could have more time . . . time to convince Fredericka that Image was a horse worth keeping.

4

SIDE BY SIDE IMAGE AND STAR JOGGED CLOCKWISE AROUND the track, Image against the outside rail. Melanie posted in the saddle, feeling tense. She held the left rein taut and kept her right heel in the filly's side. Still, Image sidestepped to the right, trying to get closer to Star. One of her ears was cocked toward him, and her right eye rolled as she cast suspicious glances at the chestnut colt.

"Stop it," Melanie scolded. She kept envisioning Image's bared teeth sinking into the flesh of Star's neck, or worse, Image freaking out and crashing through the railing. The filly *had* to learn to get used to other horses or she'd never race.

It was Saturday, and morning works had been over an hour before. Melanie had wanted to take her time with Image, so she'd waited until the track was empty.

"So far so good," Christina said when they trotted past the quarter pole. But Melanie wasn't so sure. The filly felt like a coiled spring, ready to lurch forward at any moment.

Suddenly Image swished her tail and swung her hindquarters toward Star as if about to kick. "No!" Melanie said firmly. She dug her heels into the filly's sides, collected her, and made her step sideways away from Star, who only flicked his ears calmly.

Christina chuckled. "Quit worrying. Star can handle himself. Once more around and I bet she forgets about him."

"Not likely," Melanie said through clenched teeth. "She's watching every move Star makes. I think she's worried he's going to get one step ahead of her."

"If she's that competitive, she'll be hard to beat."

"True, but I don't want her killing the competition, either."

Christina laughed, but Melanie didn't join in. She was serious. Plus it was taking every ounce of her energy and attention to keep Image focused. If they could get around the oval that day with no problems, their next jaunt together would be easier.

Circling, they trotted counterclockwise. Melanie could still tell the filly was on edge.

When they reached the gap, the two horses slowed to a walk. Melanie was soaked with sweat despite the chilly air. Her side ached with a stitch, and her legs and arms felt like jelly. Image's neck glistened with sweat, and her mouth frothed. Melanie patted her soothingly, but the filly tossed her head, still keyed up. Meanwhile, Christina and Star looked totally relaxed and refreshed.

"The problem is, she's using all her energy worrying about the other horses," Melanie gasped, trying to catch her breath. "She'll never win if she can't concentrate on running. And I'll be too exhausted from fighting her to ride properly."

"She'll get used to it. Let's give them a break Sunday, then do this all next week," Christina suggested. "When she's used to Star, we'll try it with Raven or one of the other fillies. Then we'll try it with two other fillies." Halting Star, Christina gave her cousin a reassuring smile. "You forget what great progress she's made since this summer," she reminded Melanie. "So keep being patient. That's what got you this far."

"You're right." Melanie nodded. They went through the gap, and she dismounted, her legs buckling. For a second she leaned against Image's side, feeling the rhythmic rise and fall of the horse's ribs. Image *was* doing great, Melanie thought. She was glad Christina had said so. The day before, the filly had again balked at the starting gate. After half an hour of patient coaxing, she'd walked through. But that morning Image had planted her hooves, and nothing

43

Melanie and Ian did had made any difference.

Melanie sighed. "It's just hard to stay confident," she told Christina as she ran her hand up the stirrups and loosened Image's girth. "Image seems to enjoy fighting me. What if she's not ready by the end of December? If she's going to race, she has to prove she can break from a starting gate. You know how picky Turfway's officials are. If she isn't approved by them before race day, we'll have to scratch her from the race."

"True. But you have three weeks. That should be enough time," Christina said as they headed toward the barn.

"Unless something awful happens."

Christina stopped in her tracks. "Listen to yourself! Stop being so negative, or you're going to convince yourself you and Image *can't* do it. Then Brad will win. He'll get Image. Is *that* what you want?"

Melanie's brows rose at Christina's reproachful tone. Then she realized her cousin was right. "Thanks. I guess I needed a friendly slap in the face."

Christina laughed. "And I'm just the cousin to do it."

Just then Ashleigh hurried up, looking concerned.

"We're cooling the horses off, Aunt Ashleigh," Melanie said quickly.

"I came out to tell you that Fredericka and Vince are here," Ashleigh said to Melanie. "They're waiting for you in the office. I told them to wait and I'd find you."

"Vince Jones?" Melanie asked stupidly, as if there were another Vince besides Fredericka's trainer.

"What does he want?" Christina asked.

"I'm not sure." Ashleigh slanted her eyes toward Melanie. "But I think it has something to do with Image's first race."

Melanie relaxed. "Oh. Well, he *is* Fredericka's trainer. I guess he has to be involved."

"Mel, I know you and Vince haven't exactly seen eye to eye," Ashleigh said, falling into step beside Melanie as she led Image toward the training barn. "But he does have a lot of experience. And even though Image is at Whitebrook, he's still officially her trainer."

Melanie and Vince had butted heads many times over Image's training. Vince had even ordered her to stay away from Image and his barn. But Melanie had slowly won over the gruff trainer after she had proven that she really was the best person to work with the spoiled filly.

"Don't worry," Melanie reassured her aunt. "I promise not to bite Vince's head off. As soon as I give Image a bath, I'll come in and talk with them."

"Get Dani to walk her when you're done with her bath," Ashleigh said. "I'll tell them you'll be there in ten minutes."

When Ashleigh left, Melanie and Christina led the horses into the barn. "This is so exciting, Mel," Christina said, hooking Star to crossties. "Image's first race. Can you believe it's finally happening?"

"No." Melanie shook her head. Unbuckling the girth, she slid the saddle and pad off. The filly's back was dark with sweat, her belly matted with dirt. "I've dreamed about it a hundred times, that's for sure." She glanced over at Christina. "Yesterday Ian and I checked Turfway's schedule for December thirtieth. There's a race called the Holiday Maiden that sounds perfect for Image. I hope that's the one Vince has in mind."

Leading Image into the heated washroom, Melanie hooked her to crossties. While she adjusted the water temperature, she couldn't help smiling dreamily. She'd been fantasizing about racing Image since she'd first met the powerful filly. Now it was actually going to happen. Sure, there was a lot left to do—getting Image approved by the track officials was the biggest step. But if Vince was at Whitebrook, he must be confident that Image would be ready, too.

"Ouch!" Melanie exclaimed as the filly whipped her with her tail. Spinning, she gave her a stern look. "Okay. I wasn't paying attention to you for one second. Now I am!" She turned the hose on Image, letting the warm water soak her from head to hoof. Image danced and kicked as the water trickled down her sides. Then she shook like a dog, spraying Melanie.

After shutting off the hose, Melanie used the sweat scraper to whisk off the excess water. Then she rubbed the filly vigorously, using up several towels. When Image was almost dry, Melanie covered her with two layers of blankets.

"Dani's going to walk you, so behave," she instructed as she led Image from the washroom. Dani met her in the aisle. "I think she's pretty tired," Melanie told the groom. "With any luck, she won't give you a hard time."

Dani took the lead shank a little hesitantly. The groom was great with horses, but she wasn't used to dealing with Image. "We'll stay in the barn," Dani said. "That way if she pulls away and gets loose, she won't go far."

Melanie thanked the groom, then hurried down the aisle to the office, located at the far end of the barn. As she approached, she heard voices through the closed door. She paused. Her sweatshirt and jeans were wet, and her hair was plastered on her head from wearing her helmet. She scraped the manure off her boot soles and ran her fingers through her blond hair, trying to fluff it up. There wasn't anything she could do about her damp, smelly clothes.

Opening the door, she stepped inside and greeted Vince and Fredericka. The trainer wore his usual khaki pants, tweed sport coat, and gruff expression. Fredericka was impeccably dressed in a blue wool suit with matching leather pumps, handbag, and gloves.

As soon as Melanie came in, Ashleigh stood up. "I'll be in the broodmare barn if you need me," she said.

"If I need you?" Melanie glanced around, noticing Fredericka's strained expression. "What's going on?" she asked, instantly alert.

Fredericka looked away. "Vince will explain."

"Image has been entered in next Saturday's maiden race," Vince said, going straight to the point. "You've got five days to get her ready for the track. Thursday the officials will watch her break from the gate. If they qualify her, she'll be in the fifth race on Saturday."

Melanie's jaw dropped. "But she won't even load in the starting gate!" she told the trainer. "You're crazy if you think she'll be ready to race by Saturday."

Vince stood up, his eyes narrowing at the word *crazy*, and Melanie cursed her runaway mouth. Vince hated anyone arguing with him, even if she was right. "It's out of your hands, Melanie," he said coldly. "We'll van her to the track Thursday morning."

"But—"

"You'll be listed as her jockey," Vince went on, cutting her off. "But keep arguing and I'll put someone else on her."

Melanie snapped her mouth shut.

"Fredericka, I'll meet you at the car," Vince said.

Hat in hand, he strode past Melanie and out of the office, shutting the door forcefully behind him.

Melanie stared at the closed door in stunned horror. Had she heard Vince right? Was he serious about running Image so soon?

Slowly she turned to face Fredericka. The apologetic expression on the older woman's face answered Melanie's question. Vince was serious.

Image had seven days.

5

MELANIE DROPPED DOWN IN THE CHAIR VINCE HAD BEEN sitting in, her legs rubbery. Fredericka was still staring at her lap.

"Fredericka, what's going on? You know Image isn't ready. What is Vince talking about?"

"Don't blame Vince. He's only trying to help me," Fredericka said. Fanning out the fingers of her right hand, she pulled off her glove. "The bank won't wait. They want their money now. Image needs to prove she can win races or I have to sell her."

"But I thought you had connections at the bank," Melanie protested. "You were going to talk to the board of directors."

Fredericka's laugh sounded hollow. "Oh, wasn't I the naive one? I soon discovered that everyone I knew on the board is either retired or dead. The new directors don't care about a foolish old lady who squandered all her money on racehorses. They only care about profits. Not that I blame them." When she raised her eyes, she looked resigned but determined. "I won't lose my farm, Melanie. Charles and I bought that farm together. It's all I've got left."

"But why does Image have to race next weekend? It's too soon."

"I know you don't believe it, but Vince doesn't want Image to fail, either," Fredericka said. "He's looked carefully at every maiden race this month. The Holiday Maiden, which is at the end of December, has a large purse. It's attracting fillies all the way from New York. That means there will be a big field, with lots of two-year-olds that have raced before. Since it will be her first race, Image could be crushed by the competition. On the other hand, next Saturday's races traditionally have low attendance because they're so close to the Christmas holidays. Everybody's shopping and decorating. Vince predicts there will be a small field in the race he's picked for Image. He knows several trainers who are entering fillies that have never raced before. It would be the perfect practice race for my princess."

Melanie had watched races where most of the entries were first-time runners. Two-year-olds were gangly, still growing babies, and their first races were comical. Half the time the horses broke from the gate at

51

a trot—if they broke at all. Some stood frozen in the starting gate, traumatized by the sounds and sights. Others tripped over their own legs; still others balked until their jockeys whipped them forward. Those that finally ran zigzagged down the track, bumping awkwardly into each other.

Melanie tapped her lip, thinking. Vince might not be so crazy after all. If she could get Image to break halfway decently from the gate and move forward, they might have a chance at winning.

"So winning or placing in *any* race will make the bankers happy?" Melanie asked.

Fredericka nodded. "They know the horse business is risky. They only want assurance that I'll be able to keep paying off my debts. They don't care how I—or, rather, how *Image* earns the money."

"Sounds like I don't have any choice," Melanie said, standing up. "And it sounds like I owe Vince an apology."

Fredericka tilted her head. "He really does want Image to succeed."

"I'll walk you to your car," Melanie said. They left the office and started down the aisle. Dani was leading Image toward them. As they passed each stall the filly glared at any horse who dared hang its head over the stall guard.

Melanie and Fredericka sighed simultaneously, like tired parents, and then laughed at their shared reaction.

52

"We must be thinking the same thing," Melanie said.

"Yes. You have your work cut out for you, Melanie," Fredericka said.

Melanie swallowed hard as she felt a heavy weight settle on her shoulders. She was Image's trainer *and* her jockey. It was her responsibility to get Image ready for the race. It was her responsibility to ride her to a win.

And she only had a week.

Sunday morning Melanie woke early. The sky was dark and her bedside clock said 6:03. She lay in bed, her stomach churning. The day wouldn't be a vacation for Image after all. There was too much to do.

Groaning, Melanie pulled the quilt over her face. How was she going to pull it off?

She was only sixteen. She wasn't really a trainer, she'd never ridden a horse in its very first race, and she only had six days.

But that wasn't the worst of it.

If she failed, Image would be sold.

Tears trickled down Melanie's cheek, dotting the quilt. Christina had told her to quit being negative, but she couldn't help it. She couldn't find one positive thing about the situation.

Not one.

"Mel, are you under there?"

Melanie whipped the quilt off her face. Her cousin

was sitting on the edge of her bed, staring down at her. She was dressed in her riding clothes.

"Christina! You scared me. What are you doing up? It's Sunday. You get to sleep in."

"I'm going to help you with Image. Didn't Kevin tell you?"

"Tell me what?"

Christina rolled her eyes. "I should have known he'd forget."

The night before, Christina had been out with Parker. Around ten Kevin had stopped by to watch some TV with her after his date with his girlfriend, Lindsey, but he hadn't said anything about Sunday, and Melanie had gone to bed before her cousin came home.

"Kevin was supposed to tell you that we'd help with Image today. He's going to ride Thunder Bones and I'll ride Star. We'll work the three of them together in one of the pastures."

Melanie propped herself up on one elbow. "But you shouldn't have to work on Sunday."

Christina grinned. "It won't be work." Standing up, she pulled a sweatshirt from the back of a chair and tossed it to Melanie. "It'll be fun. See you downstairs."

When she left, Melanie wiped her eyes. She was glad Christina hadn't seen her tears—or at least hadn't said anything about them. She didn't want Chris to know how worried she was. Throwing back the quilt, she grabbed her riding clothes and got dressed. When she hurried downstairs, she was feeling better. Knowing Christina and Kevin were going to help her made all the difference.

Half an hour later she was riding Image between Star and Thunder Bones up the frost-covered hill behind the barns. The filly was all puffed up like an angry cat, walking stiff-legged with a hump in her back, and when Melanie squeezed her into a trot, she ducked her head and crow-hopped.

"She hates being between you guys, so watch out," Melanie warned Kevin and Christina. "She's liable to explode any minute."

"Go ahead and steer her toward me," Kevin said. "Thunder Bones will take care of her." Thunder Bones was an older racehorse with an unflappable disposition, who had raced for nine years. He was often ridden with the young colts and fillies. When Image pinned her ears and crowded into him, Thunder Bones calmly reached over and bit her on the neck.

Startled, Image shied sideways, crashing into Star, who just kept trotting steadily forward. The filly stumbled, throwing Melanie onto her neck. Quickly Melanie righted herself, collected Image, and made her trot. Image tossed her head angrily, resisting Melanie's aids. But when she fell behind the other horses, she quickly lengthened her stride to catch up.

Kevin grinned at Melanie. "Bet she won't try that again!"

For twenty minutes they trotted uphill and down. By the time Kevin raised his arm, signaling them to walk, all three horses and riders were blowing.

"This is doing Star a world of good!" Christina said breathlessly. "Just what he needs to get back in shape."

Glancing over at the chestnut colt, Melanie nodded in agreement. Star's muscles rippled, and his coat shone with golden-red lights.

"Well, us old guys have had it." Kevin was leaning over the pommel, panting loudly. Melanie laughed. She knew he was faking. Kevin had just finished the fall soccer season and was in super shape.

"Once Image settled down, it felt pretty good," Melanie admitted. She patted Image's damp neck. The filly's ears were pricked. For once her attention was on where they were going instead of who was beside her. "But it's a long way from breezing around a track. I need some suggestions on what to do differently with Image when we take her to Turfway on Thursday. You know how she hates the track."

"I don't think you should worry, Mel. She's a different horse since the last time she was there," Christina said as they circled the pasture.

"Really, she hasn't tried to kill anyone since she's been at Whitebrook," Kevin teased.

"Be serious. What if she starts acting crazy again?"

Christina halted Star at the gate. "She won't. You'll be there to make sure she's okay."

"Then what if I can't get her loaded in the starting gate?"

"That's what we're going to work on this morning," Kevin said. "Dad and I thought a little competition might get the princess to load. He's meeting us down there."

Kevin rode Thunder Bones from the pasture. As Melanie steered Image after him, she chewed her lip, still worrying

"Why don't you ask Vince if you can stable Image in Whitebrook's stalls instead of his barn?" Kevin suggested. "There won't be as much commotion."

Big trainers like Vince rented an entire barn at the track and kept horses there for the whole season. Whitebrook had a small group of stalls because only the horses that were running would be stabled at Turfway. After their races, they'd be vanned back to Whitebrook.

Melanie brightened. "Great idea. Chris, do you think Ashleigh would let Pirate come to Turfway, too? If we stabled him next to Image, he might help calm her."

"It depends on how many horses Whitebrook is running next weekend," Christina said. "But I have a feeling Mom'll say yes. She knows this race is important."

The three riders rode through the gap and onto the

track. Ian was waiting by the starting gate. Melanie's pulse quickened. Breaking clean from the gate was crucial. She only wished she had four *weeks* to work on it instead of four *days*.

"Christina, you and Kevin walk your horses through the chutes," Ian said when they came up. "See if Image will get the idea."

Thunder Bones walked through chute three, and Star walked through chute five.

Melanie aimed Image toward chute four. The filly's ears flicked wildly as the two horses continued down the track. Finally she could stand it no longer. She lunged through the chute and out the other side, then charged down the track at a gallop, passing the two horses.

Melanie sawed on the reins, finally stopping the filly at the far turn. It was a crummy break, Melanie knew, but at least it was a start.

The second time, Ian had the front doors of the chutes closed. Image balked, but when she saw the other two horses standing quietly in chutes three and five, she finally walked in.

Melanie said a silent thank-you. It was the first time Image had been in the starting gate next to other horses. Rigid, she rolled her eyes to the right, then the left. Melanie fed her a treat and soothed her with soft words.

"I'm going to ring the bell and open the front stall

doors as if it were a race," Ian said, "but keep your horses at a walk. Melanie, you be ready for anything."

Nodding tensely, Melanie grabbed a hunk of mane. When the bell rang and the front gates opened, Image was so startled, she almost fell onto her knees. Melanie pitched onto the filly's neck, losing her grip on the reins.

Image ducked her head between her legs and bucked wildly, throwing Melanie in the air. Melanie tumbled to the ground, rolling away unhurt. Whinnying with delight, Image raced down the track riderless. Melanie stood up, brushed off her jeans, and looked up at her friends. Kevin and Christina were trying hard not to smile.

Image cantered a sharp U-turn, raced back, and skidded to a stop in front of Melanie. She snatched up the reins. "That is not funny!" she scolded the filly. Throwing her head in the air, Image snorted and rolled her eyes like a wild horse.

"Okay, let's try that again," Ian said, his hand in front of his mouth as if he, too, was trying not to laugh.

He gave Melanie a leg up, and she steered Image to the other side of the starting gate. This time Image walked eagerly into the chute. Melanie knew why, too. Image had decided the whole chute thing was fun— especially the part where she got to toss Melanie.

"But this time I'm going to be ready," Melanie said between clenched teeth. When the gates snapped open, Image leaped out and began to buck once more. Melanie sat deep. Using a pulley rein and all her strength, she yanked the filly's head up and around. Image gave one more stiff-legged hop, then turned in a tight circle. Finally she stopped when she realized she couldn't go anywhere.

Melanie caught her breath. Kevin began clapping. "We'd like to congratulate the winner of the White-brook Rodeo—Melanie Graham, with a record thirteen seconds," he announced in a Texas twang.

Everybody laughed.

"Good riding, Melanie," Ian said, chuckling. "Now let's try that again—only not quite so dramatic this time."

The third time the gate opened, Image bolted out and cantered a few rough strides until Melanie turned her in a circle once again. The fourth time, the filly broke quietly, and the three horses trotted down the track.

"And Thunder Bones, ridden by the handsome Kevin McLean, is in the lead," Kevin said, this time in the nasal voice of a track announcer. "Wonder's Star, recently designated a has-been, is trotting briskly on the rail. Image, ridden by Melanie 'Cowgirl' Graham, is making her move on the outside. And what a move it is—that filly's got a ten-speed trot!"

When the three horses crossed the finish line, Melanie collapsed in laughter.

"It's about time you cheered up, Mel," Chris said.

"We've got a couple more days to practice breaking from the gate. I know there's a lot of pressure on you, but you and Image can do it. I know you can."

Melanie steered Image beside Star. Kevin walked on her other side. "We've got to," she declared grimly. But then she smiled at her friends. "Hey, thank you, guys. That was way more fun than I thought it would be."

Thursday morning Joe drove the van through Turfway's gates and down the drive to the shed row where Whitebrook's stalls were located. As the van swayed around corners Melanie sat rigid in the passenger seat, listening to Image carry on. They'd brought Pirate along for company, but the filly had still whinnied and stomped the whole trip.

Melanie had taken the day off from school. Neither Ashleigh or Mike was happy with the idea—schoolwork came first—but Melanie had convinced them that she had no choice. She needed to spend the entire day at Turfway.

When Joe parked, Melanie let out a sigh. "Image is *not* happy. Let's hope she settles down."

"When are they clocking her?" Joe asked.

"Nine. Vince picked a time when the track would be fairly empty. Then at noon the starter is going to watch her break from the gate. Should be fun," Melanie said sarcastically.

Joe laughed. "Just remember, every two-year-old

has to prove it can break from the gate. And they all have to run that first race. Some survive." He shrugged. "And some don't."

"That's encouraging." Melanie swung open her door and jumped from the van. She helped Joe lower the heavy ramp. Image was in the stall closest to the door. She tossed her head, rattling the chains, her eyes wide as she stared at the backside activity. Dazzle and Rhapsody were in the stalls opposite Image and Pirate. The two three-year-olds were also racing on Saturday.

Climbing the ramp, Melanie snapped the lead line to Image's halter, then undid the crossties. Image wore leg wraps, bell boots, a head protector, and a blue-and-white blanket. Melanie wasn't taking any chances on the filly hurting herself.

"Walk easy," she crooned. With a snort, Image barreled past Melanie, dragging her down the ramp. When they reached the bottom, the filly threw up her head and whinnied challengingly. A dozen horses whinnied back.

Melanie groaned.

"At least she's not quivering with fear," Joe said, chuckling.

Melanie led Image to the stall that she and Kevin had fixed up the night before. Kevin had knocked out a wall, making it a double stall, and hung a metal mesh top door, which they could close if Image showed any signs of trying to break out.

Melanie led the filly into the stall, shutting the door behind her. Immediately Image whirled and stuck her head over the bottom door. Then she banged it impatiently with her foreleg. "Just cool it," Melanie said, trying not to get annoyed. The filly was trampling all over her, and they hadn't even been at Turfway five minutes. "I've got to help Joe unload the other horses."

Unhooking the lead, Melanie opened the door and squeezed around it. Image lunged for the opening, but Melanie slammed the door and threw the latch. "Locked. Now just hang tight. I'll be back to tack you up. Save that energy for your timed works."

Which will be a joke, Melanie thought as she headed back to the van. Image had never galloped on a real track carrying a rider. She'd only run away after *dumping* her rider. But things were moving so fast, Melanie had no choice. In one hour she would be racing Image on the track while the official clocker timed her. *Anything* could happen.

"You've done this hundreds of times," Vince told Melanie as he walked beside her and Image.

"But not on Image," Melanie said tersely. "And not when so much is at stake."

Vince didn't say anything. To him, this was just one more horse preparing for one more race. To Melanie, it was *everything*. A horse had to have a recorded work in order to be eligible to race. If Image couldn't get past Turfway's officials, she couldn't race. And if she didn't race . . .

Melanie pushed the horrible thought out of her head. Her grip tightened on the reins as the filly pranced down the path to Turfway's track. Vince kept his fingers lightly on the horse's neck, as if trying to keep her from exploding.

"Image isn't any more high-strung than most maiden fillies," Vince said.

Yeah, right, Melanie thought. Vince hadn't been on Image all the times she'd turned into a bucking bronco.

When they reached the track, Melanie was glad to see it was empty except for a few last-minute stragglers who were cooling off their horses. Tony, the gap outrider, waited at the gate, smoking a cigarette as he slouched in the saddle.

"Morning, Vince," he mumbled, his cigarette bobbing between his lips. "This the filly?" He nodded toward Image.

Vince nodded back. Melanie arched her brow. "What do you mean, is this the filly?"

When Vince didn't say anything, Melanie frowned. "If you think she'll be fine, then why did you warn Tony there might be trouble?"

Tony chuckled. "There's always trouble with young ones."

Melanie had to admit that Tony was right. The

maidens often dumped their riders, stumbled over their own feet, or crashed into each other. She needed to stop being so defensive. If Vince had warned the outrider, it was only because he didn't want anyone to get hurt.

"Let me worry about my job, Melanie," Vince growled sternly. "You worry about riding Image. You've done a good job with her these last weeks. She's got great breeding. Now it's her turn to show us what she can do."

"Right." Relaxing her grip on the reins, Melanie steered Image through the gap, then walked her in a circle while Vince gave her his instructions. "Jog her to the eighth pole, breeze to the half-mile to warm her up, then work a half mile."

Melanie nodded. "Got it." Vince walked over to where the gap clocker was standing with his stopwatch and walkie-talkie.

"Black filly named Perfect Image," Vince told the gap clocker, who relayed the information to the official clocker, who would do the actual timing. "She'll gallop four furlongs from the half-mile pole."

Melanie heard the squawk of the walkie-talkie as she squeezed Image into a trot. Her heart was pounding, but the filly seemed calm enough. Her strides were bouncy, throwing Melanie around in the saddle, and her head was high as she took in the sights and sounds.

When they reached the eighth pole Melanie trotted Image across the track to the inside railing and headed counterclockwise. "This is it, Image," Melanie said. "This time it's official. You're doing great. No matter what happens, just remember that I'm here for you."

At the three-eighths pole Melanie put her weight in her stirrups, sat forward, and urged the filly into a canter. Image tossed her head and broke easily, her stride rocking and eager. She flicked her ears, listening as Melanie kept talking: "I'm more nervous than you, but we can do it. I know we can. This is what we've been training for."

As the half-mile pole loomed closer Melanie hunkered lower on Image's neck and made a kissing noise. "Go, girl. Do it!"

For a second the filly hesitated, as if confused. Melanie pumped with her hands. "Go! Run! This is what you've been waiting for!"

Image's ears flicked back and forth nervously. Then she lengthened her stride just a little, as if testing Melanie out. When Melanie clucked again, the filly's stride grew stronger and they blew past the half-mile pole.

As they galloped down the empty track, Melanie gasped. She could feel the power as Image's legs pounded the ground. She could hear the filly's rhythmic, effortless breathing. If Image had suddenly risen into the air like a plane taking off from a runway,

Melanie wouldn't have been surprised. The filly was so fast and so smooth that it felt as if she were flying.

The cold air stung Melanie's eyes. The wind brushed her cheeks. Exhilaration filled her, and she grinned with excitement.

The finish line flew by so suddenly that Melanie almost missed it. Her fingers were numb and her teeth chattered, but she didn't care.

She wanted to gallop Image forever.

6

Melanie caught sight of the outrider cantering toward them, and she came back to earth. "You and that filly okay?" Tony yelled.

"We're great! Just *great!*" Melanie hollered back. Standing in the stirrups, she signaled Image to slow. Before the filly dropped to a trot, she gave a playful buck, tossing Melanie onto her neck. Grabbing mane, Melanie laughed. She knew exactly how Image felt.

"Didn't I tell you that you'd love racing once you tried it?" she teased the black filly.

The outrider trotted his pony beside them. Reaching over, he grabbed the dangling rein. "Didn't want you getting tossed off," he said, grinning. "Nice work. No wonder Vince wanted you galloping on an empty track."

"What do you mean?" Melanie asked.

Tony tapped his helmet. "I've watched enough horses run, I got a clock in my head. This filly was so fast, I'll bet Vince didn't want the other trainers to see her run."

Melanie's eyes widened. She'd been so caught up with the joy of galloping Image, she'd forgotten all about their time. Her pulse quickened. Had Image been that fast?

They jogged slowly around the track until Image's breathing was even, then walked to the gap. Vince was writing something in his workout book.

"Whoa." Halting Image, Melanie slid off. She thanked Tony. He tipped his hat and then rode off. Still Vince didn't look up.

Turning, Melanie lowered the girth a hole, then felt Image's chest. She glanced at Vince, quickly looking away before he noticed. She needed to walk Image, take off the rundowns, check her legs to make sure they were cool, bathe her, walk her again, then let her relax and eat some hay.

But she didn't want to leave until she found out how good their time had been.

She cleared her throat, hoping to get Vince's attention. "Uh, how was our time?" she asked.

Vince chuckled and shook his head.

Melanie wasn't sure she'd heard right. Vince Jones? Chuckling?

"She did four furlongs in forty-two seconds," he finally said. "That's better than most of my colts."

Melanie's face broke into a huge grin. She flung her arms around Image's neck. "I knew she could do it!"

Image rubbed her itchy face on Melanie's sleeve. "Okay, I get the hint. Bath time." Pulling the reins over the filly's head, Melanie started walking her toward the barn. She couldn't stop smiling—not just because of the fast time, but because galloping Image had felt so amazing.

Vince fell into step beside her. "You two looked good out there. How did she feel?"

"Like she could fly. Now, if she can just break from the gate . . . ," Melanie said, her smile changing to a frown.

"I've got to look after my other horses. I'll see you there at noon," Vince said, and walked briskly away.

When Vince disappeared around the corner of the barn, Melanie let her shoulders sag. She'd been so excited about the fast time that she hadn't realized how exhausted she was. Unsnapping her helmet, she looked around for Joe or Dani. She wanted to tell someone the great news about Image, but no one else was there.

Sighing, she tossed her helmet on an empty chair by Image's stall, then bent over and started unwinding a muddy leg wrap. The great news would have to wait. There was too much work to do before noon.

• • •

"Forty-two seconds!" Ashleigh repeated excitedly. It was eleven-thirty. Ashleigh had volunteered to ride Pirate and pony Image to the starting gate for her test. Now she was holding Image while Melanie tightened the web girth. "That's a terrific time. You should be proud of her."

"I'm not getting too cocky until the official starter approves her," Melanie said. "You know how awful she's been breaking from the gate. For some reason, she thinks she's a bronc in a rodeo."

Ashleigh ran her palm down the filly's face. "She'll do great. Won't you, Image?" she said, giving the filly a stern look. Image shook her head and snorted.

Melanie laughed. "That look may work on me when I haven't done my homework, Aunt Ashleigh. But I don't think it made an impression on Image." Stooping, she again checked the filly's padded leg wraps, making sure they covered her legs from the knees to the top of her hooves. The last thing she needed was a banged-up horse.

She was about to mount when Ashleigh asked, "Aren't you forgetting something?"

"I've got my helmet."

"You need to put on a protective vest. There's one in the tack trunk."

Melanie knew not to argue with Ashleigh. Besides, her aunt was right. She'd seen horses flip over on top jockeys in the gate.

Pulling off her jacket, Melanie slipped on the vest and fastened the Velcro tabs. Butterflies tickled her stomach, and her palms were sweating. She closed her eyes, visualizing a perfect break from the gate. She'd read about the visualization technique in a sports magazine. She'd try anything to make sure Image got approved.

Ten minutes later Ashleigh and Pirate were ponying them to the starting gate. Another horse and rider waited beside it. Melanie recognized Fred Anderson, who rode for a trainer named Jimmy J. He was riding a long-legged gray colt.

"Hey, Mel, is that Image?" Fred asked. Fred was an apprentice jockey, just like Melanie. They were friends and had even dated once.

"Yeah, it's the bad-luck filly herself," Melanie said, repeating the name the other grooms and jockeys had given Image. She glanced up, spotting Vince and the official starter in the starter's tower.

"Let's hope she'll bring us both good luck," Fred said as one of the gate crew came over.

Taking hold of the bridle, the assistant starter walked Fred's colt into the chute. The colt was halfway in when he suddenly backed out and whirled toward Image. She pinned her ears and lunged at him, but Ashleigh held the lead line taut. The second time the colt loaded easily, and the crew slammed the gate against his rump.

Ashleigh circled Image, then unhooked the lead line. Melanie urged the filly forward until she faced an open chute. "Just pretend we're at Whitebrook," she whispered.

The assistant starter tried to grab the left rein, and Image threw up her head. "See if she'll walk in by herself," Melanie suggested.

The starter backed away. For what seemed like forever, Image stood there, swishing her tail. Melanie kicked her lightly, but she didn't budge. Melanie glanced up at the starter's tower. Vince had a bored expression on his face. The starter was checking his watch. Fred's colt kicked the side of the chute.

Melanie exhaled, not sure what to do. Then, suddenly, Image walked into the stall. When the gates closed behind her, she jumped nervously.

Melanie gave her a soothing pat. "No bucking-bronco routines, okay?"

Leaning forward, Melanie balanced lightly in the saddle. The bell rang, and the front doors flew open. Image leaped from the stall and began to buck. Melanie jerked the filly's head up. Then she kicked her hard, and Image leaped forward and began to charge down the track. Melanie made a bridge with the reins and let Image run. When the filly began to puff, Melanie used her voice and body to slow her.

They were almost back to the starting gate when the filly finally broke into a trot. Fred and his colt were ambling down the homestretch, heading to the backside.

Melanie's chest felt tight. Image hadn't been terrible, but she hadn't done too well, either. Then she spotted Ashleigh and Pirate jogging clockwise to meet them. Ashleigh had a big smile on her face.

Melanie's eyes widened. "Does that smile mean we were approved?" she called when Ashleigh rode closer.

"Sure does." Ashleigh pulled Pirate up beside them. "The starter said Image wasn't a danger to herself or others. Plus he was impressed with your ability to handle her."

Melanie whooped. "I can't believe it, Aunt Ashleigh. You know what that means—Image and I are really racing this Saturday!"

When Melanie got home from Turfway that night, it was after nine o'clock. Dani was still at the track, spending the night on a cot in the tack room so she could keep an eye on Image, Dazzle, and Rhapsody. Melanie hated leaving Image, but Ashleigh had reminded Melanie that there was school on Friday and insisted she come home.

After eating a tuna sandwich, Melanie soaked in a hot bubble bath, changed into a nightshirt, and padded downstairs to the family room. She wanted to call her father and tell him the good news.

"Dad, guess what! Image is racing this weekend!" Settling back against the sofa cushions, Melanie told him everything that had happened in the past week. The fact that Melanie was a jockey made Will nervous, but he was always happy to hear his daughter's stories.

"Wow, that was fast," Will said. "I thought you weren't going to race her until the end of the month."

"I didn't have any choice." Melanie explained Fredericka's dilemma.

"Do you think Image will be ready for Saturday's race?" Will asked.

"Well, after today, I'm feeling a little more confident. Image still isn't happy at the track, but Pirate's with her, and Kevin took out a partition to make a double stall, so she has plenty of room."

Will chuckled. "Nothing's too good for the princess."

"And Image ran four furlongs in forty-two seconds!" There was a long silence, and Melanie giggled. "That's fast, Dad."

"Oh, right. I wasn't sure whether I was supposed to be happy or sad," Will joked.

"Vince said it's faster than most of his colts."

Will whistled. "Hey, how about if your old man comes to watch you race?"

"Um . . ." Melanie hesitated. She already had as much pressure as she could stand.

"Hey, you know I love you whether you win, lose, or fall off," Will teased.

Melanie laughed. "In that case, I'd love for you to come."

"I'm flying to Atlanta tomorrow to meet a prospective client and his band," Will said. He owned Graham Productions, a company that promoted and managed musical groups. "I can finish my business that day and fly in late Friday night. I'll stay at a hotel near the track."

"Sounds great," Melanie said, excited at the prospect of seeing her father again. "I'll let Ashleigh and Mike know."

They said goodbye, and Melanie hung up. She wished she could see more of her dad, but his business and life were in New York City, while her life was in Kentucky. She missed him, since for most of her life it had been just her and her dad—her mom, Mike Reese's sister, had died when Melanie was young. He had remarried a few years before, and he and Susan, her stepmom, were able to visit often.

Closing her eyes, Melanie rested her head against the sofa back. She needed to go to bed, but her nerves were still on edge. She glanced at the clock. It was almost ten. She hoped Image was okay. Dani had promised to check her often and report to Melanie if the filly didn't settle.

Just then the phone rang. Melanie grabbed the

receiver and heard Dani's panicky voice babbling into her ear.

"Wait, slow down," Melanie said. "I can't understand you."

"Melanie, you've got to come quick. There's something wrong with Image!"

7

MELANIE'S HEART LEAPED INTO HER THROAT. "WHAT DO
you mean, something's wrong? Is she sick?"

"No, nothing like that. She just won't settle down,"
Dani explained, her voice rising. "She's pacing her
stall and kicking the door hard, and I can't get her to
quit. I'm scared she's going to pull a tendon or bruise
her—"

"I'll be right over," Melanie cut in. "Just make sure
her doors are secure. I don't want her breaking out!"
She jumped up and ran outside to the McLeans' house
down the driveway.

"Thanks for driving me to Turfway," Melanie said to
Kevin as they sped to the racetrack. "I know it's late."

"Stop thanking me. I want to make sure Image is all

78

right, too," Kevin said, his attention on the highway as he wove his pickup truck through the traffic.

Melanie shivered. The truck hadn't warmed up, and she was icy cold. She'd been in such a hurry to leave, she hadn't worn a coat.

"I've got an extra jacket and a blanket in the truck bed," Kevin offered. "For emergencies."

"Image is one big emergency," Melanie grumbled. "*I* should have stayed there tonight, not Dani. She's not used to Image and her tantrums. But what if Image never gets used to the track? I can't baby-sit for her all the time."

Kevin shrugged. "A lot of racehorses have quirks. When I was nine, my father trained a colt named Special Day, who was in love with a chicken. If we didn't bring that chicken to the track, Special Day refused to come out of his stall. And forget racing." Kevin chuckled. "Guess who got to be the chicken handler? I still have scars where that stupid bird pecked me."

"Image would probably eat the chicken for dinner," Melanie said gloomily.

"Don't worry, Mel. Image has you. That's more than enough."

Melanie was grateful for Kevin's kindness, but she wasn't sure if she really believed what he'd said. She gnawed a fingernail nervously. If she didn't stop worrying about Image, she was going to go nuts.

"So how's Lindsey?" Melanie asked, abruptly

changing the subject. She was so desperate to take her mind off her worries that she was even willing to hear about Kevin's girlfriend.

"Okay."

"Just okay?"

"We had a big argument after school."

"About what?"

"She wanted me to come over to her house after her basketball practice. I didn't want to, and she blew up. I think the problem is that Lindsey wants to get serious."

"And you don't?"

He shook his head. "I'm only seventeen. Next year we'll be headed to different colleges. I like Lindsey a lot, but I don't want to be with her every minute."

"I agree. Serious relationships are out for me, too."

Kevin started laughing.

"What? Just because I haven't dated since we broke up doesn't mean I can't have an opinion about relationships?"

"What about Fred?" Kevin teased.

"You know we're just friends." Melanie slid down in the passenger seat. The truck heater had kicked in, and she was suddenly feeling warm. She wondered what would happen if Kevin and Lindsey broke up. Would she want to date him again?

Nah. She didn't even have to think about the answer. Since they'd quit dating, she and Kevin had become great friends. She didn't want to ruin that relationship.

"Why are you looking at me like that?" Kevin asked.

"Like what?"

"Like I'm a little bacterium under a microscope."

"I was just thinking what a great friend you are," Melanie said. "And that I wouldn't want to lose you." His arm was still resting on the back of the seat, and Melanie poked it affectionately.

"Ditto," Kevin said as they pulled into Turfway's parking lot. "Okay, we're here."

Melanie swung toward the car door, instantly alert. "Drop me off at the gates. I'll meet you at the barn."

"I'll get that jacket for you," Kevin said, but Melanie was already out the door. She flashed her ID to the guard, who waved her into the backside. Since it was after ten-thirty, the area was silent and dark. By now the horses were bedded down for the night, and the night workers were either sleeping or playing cards.

Melanie jogged past the shed rows, which were illuminated by tall vapor lights. The only sounds were horses munching hay and people laughing. But as she neared Whitebrook's stalls a loud banging shattered the quiet.

Melanie quickened her pace. She rounded the corner at a run, spotting Dani standing outside Image's stall. The doors were shut, top and bottom, and in the dim light Melanie could see that the wood was splintered.

"Dani, is everything okay?" Melanie asked.

"Thank goodness you're here!" Dani exclaimed. "She's been kicking and whinnying since you left. The night man in the barn next door started complaining— I didn't know what to do!"

"You did the right thing. Thanks for calling me." Stepping up to the top door, Melanie peered into the stall. Image lunged at her, teeth bared. Surprised, Melanie jumped back, closing the door in the filly's face. Her teeth hit the door so hard, Melanie could hear the wood split.

"You can see why I didn't go in there," Dani said.

"You were smart." Melanie stepped up to the door again. "Image, it's me," she crooned. "I'm opening the door now."

This time the filly approached with her ears pricked. Melanie swung open the door and slipped inside. Image's stable blanket hung halfway off, and one of the straps was broken. Melanie laid her hand on the horse's neck, which was hot to the touch and slick with sweat.

"If we let her stand like this, she'll get sick. I'm going to have to sponge her off and then walk her until she's cool—and calmer," Melanie said. Image hated to be confined, Melanie knew, but there was nowhere to turn her out at the track. She hoped a long walk would help the filly settle down. Melanie glanced around the stall. The water bucket was smashed flat, and the hay net was still full. "She hasn't eaten?"

"Not since you left. I tried offering her a bran mash, but she dumped it over," Dani explained.

"Is she okay?" Kevin asked, hurrying up.

"Nothing a bath and walking won't cure," Melanie said. She sighed. It would be a long night.

"I'll go bridle Pirate," Kevin suggested. "We can use him to pony her. I don't want her breaking away from you and getting loose."

"Are you sure? It's bad enough I've got to be here—"

Kevin cut her off. "Of course I'm sure."

Together they gave Image a warm sponge bath and then covered her in a pile of wool coolers. Dani brought out Pirate, and Kevin leaped on him bareback. Melanie snapped three lead ropes to Image's halter rings. One she handed to Kevin. The other two she looped around Image's neck like reins. Then Dani boosted Melanie onto Image's back.

The filly danced sideways, and Melanie slid to the other side. Holding on to the blanket, she pulled herself upright. "Graceful as always," she joked.

Image took off, and Melanie had to grab her mane. Kevin snubbed the filly's head tight against his thigh, but it didn't slow her down. Eyes wide, she trotted past the shadowy shed rows as if on a mission. Finally Kevin used Pirate's bulk to push the filly through the gap in the railing and onto the track.

They trotted briskly past the grandstand, which loomed over the track, looking ghostly in the moonlight. As Melanie bounced on Image's back she stared at it with awe. She'd never been on the track when it was so silent and dark.

"Kind of spooky," she said to Kevin.

"It *is* spooky. Haven't you ever heard the story of the Turfway Terror?"

Melanie crooked one eyebrow. "There is no such thing, Kevin McLean."

"Well, don't say I didn't warn you," Kevin said, laughing eerily.

Halfway around the track Image finally slowed to a walk. "Whew," Melanie gasped. " I thought she was never going to settle down."

As they walked back to the gap Melanie let her shoulders sag. She swayed to the rhythm of Image's walk, and her eyelids drooped.

"We'd better get you back before you fall asleep," Kevin teased.

Slowly they wound their way past the shed rows. Image had relaxed enough for Kevin to slacken the lead. When they reached the barn, Melanie slid from Image's back, her feet thudding numbly on the cement floor.

Dani came out of the tack room, a blanket wrapped around her. "Can I help?" she asked, yawning.

"Thanks, but we're okay. You go on back to bed," Melanie told her.

Kevin cooled Pirate off, and Melanie hooked Image to crossties, took off the damp blankets, and groomed her.

She was so tired, she worked automatically. At some point she heard Kevin say good night, but she wasn't really sure when he left. Covering Image with a clean stable blanket, she led her back to her stall. Dani had cleaned it out and added fresh straw and water. Kevin had left a down vest and a plaid wool blanket on the chair by the stall door.

Melanie smiled sleepily. She was lucky to have friends looking out for her.

Image walked over to the hay net, snatched a bite of hay, and paced back to the stall door.

"You'd better settle down," Melanie warned her. "I don't want you tromping all over me tonight."

Throwing the down vest and wool blanket over her shoulders, Melanie secured the bottom door, then waded through the straw to a back corner. Exhausted, she wrapped the blanket around herself and sank to her knees. She plumped the vest into a pillow and set it on the straw. Snorting curiously, Image came over to see what she was doing. She sniffed Melanie from head to toe, her nostrils blowing in and out.

Melanie yawned and checked her watch. Two in the morning. No wonder she was tired. Curling into a ball, she lay down, her head cradled on the vest. The last thing she heard was Image, contentedly munching her hay.

"You are going home, Melanie," Ashleigh insisted the next morning. "To your own bed. No arguing."

Melanie had gotten up early, woken by Image's persistent nudging. After grabbing a cup of hot chocolate from the track kitchen, she'd taken Image for a long walk around the backside. They were coming back from their jaunt when Ashleigh caught up with them. Her aunt had taken one look at Melanie's haggard face and ordered her to go home.

"Mike and I are perfectly capable of baby-sitting your horse," Ashleigh said teasingly as she took the lead line from Melanie. "We have a full day of recreational activities especially planned for your difficult child—arts and crafts, a hike, songs," she added with a laugh.

Melanie was too exhausted to laugh with her. "But what if—" she began to argue.

Ashleigh raised her hand. "We can handle every what-if that comes along. Trust me."

Melanie knew her aunt was right—she needed her rest. And Image would probably be fine while she was gone as long as she got lots of attention and time out of her stall. Melanie had already told Ashleigh she was spending that night with the filly, but if she didn't get any sleep, she might fall asleep in the middle of the next day's race.

"No school?" Melanie asked hopefully.

Ashleigh rolled her eyes. "No school. But you'd better tell Christina to get your assignments."

"Thanks." Melanie gathered up her things and trudged to the tack room, where she found Dani folding up the cot. The groom had huge circles under her eyes.

"Ready to go?" Dani asked. She'd offered to drop Melanie off at Whitebrook on her way home. Dani had to be back that afternoon, too, and needed to rest up just as much as Melanie did. "You look as tired as I feel," Dani added.

"Oh, I got lots of sleep," Melanie said, trying to suppress a yawn, and the two girls giggled.

An hour later Melanie had showered, changed into a sweatshirt, and climbed into bed. She didn't remember much after that.

"Melanie!"

Startled, Melanie sat up, blinking in confusion. Then she glanced at the bedside clock. It was one o'clock in the afternoon. She'd slept for over three hours.

"Melanie! Are you up there?"

"Yes!" Throwing back the quilt, Melanie scrambled out of bed. Who kept calling? Was something wrong with Image? She flew down the hall and down the stairs, her bare feet thumping on the wooden steps. Halfway down she froze. Her father and a boy Melanie had never seen before were standing in the foyer looking up at her.

"Dad? Wh-what are you doing here?" Melanie stammered, her gaze shifting to the boy. He had shoulder-length black hair and was wearing a long black cashmere coat over a black turtleneck and black jeans. He definitely wasn't from Kentucky.

"We flew in early," Will explained. He was dressed in a camel-hair sport coat, tie, and dark brown corduroy slacks. "I called Ashleigh earlier, but she said you were probably asleep and not to call and wake you."

"Oh." Melanie glanced from her father to the other guy, who was staring at her with raised brows.

"This is Jazz Taylor, the prospective client I told you about," Will said.

Jazz smiled. He had a tan complexion and dark brown almond-shaped eyes. "Nice to meet you. Your dad told me a lot about you."

"Uh, nice to meet you." Melanie reached down and tugged at the hem of her nightshirt. "I'll be with you in a minute. I've got to change. Um, why don't you get some coffee or something?" she suggested. "You know where everything is, right, Dad?"

Turning, she thumped back up the stairs and hurried into Christina's empty bedroom. Picking up the phone, she dialed the number for the barn at the track. When no one answered, she gnawed worriedly on her lip.

Joe, Mike, and Ashleigh should all have been at the track barn. So where was everybody? Had something happened to Image? Had she pulled away from Ashleigh and run off?

A dozen horrible scenarios flashed through Melanie's mind. She had to get back to the track and find out if Image was all right.

Running into her room, she pulled clean barn clothes from her dresser drawer and got dressed. Then she stuffed a change of clothes and some toiletries into her overnight bag. Before heading downstairs, she found Christina's sleeping bag in her closet and pulled it out.

When she had everything together, she blasted downstairs and into the kitchen. Her father was starting to measure out coffee. Jazz had taken off his coat and draped it over a kitchen chair.

"Sorry, guys. No time for coffee," Melanie said as she blew past them into the mud room. Plopping her things on top of the dryer, she bent over to pull on her boots. "I need a ride to the track," she called into the kitchen. "No one's answering the phone. I'm worried that something's wrong with Image."

"I assume Image is a racehorse?" Melanie heard Jazz ask her father.

"Not just a racehorse," Will replied. "The *perfect* racehorse."

Not exactly, Melanie thought as she came back into the kitchen. The coffee can and mugs were put away, and Jazz and her father both had on their coats.

"Sorry for being in such a hurry," she apologized as she led the way to the rental car parked in front of the house. "I just need you to drop me off. Where are you staying?"

"The Windmere Hotel," Will said, opening the car door for her. She tossed her stuff into the backseat and climbed in. Jazz got into the passenger seat in front of her. One gold hoop gleamed from his earlobe.

"I'm going to the track with you," Will said when he got in. "I want to see Image, too. Besides, if I don't go to the track, I'll never get to see *you*."

"You know I love to be with you," Melanie said to her father. "But this is an emergency. Image sort of went crazy last night. I won't stop worrying until I see her for myself." Reaching over the seat, she touched her dad's shoulder. "One day you'll have to visit when there isn't a race."

"Like never?" Will joked. "Jazz, I can drop you off at the hotel if you want. It's on the way."

Jazz shook his head. "I didn't come to Kentucky to spend time in a hotel."

"When I told Jazz that Ashleigh and Mike ran a Thoroughbred farm and that you and your cousin were jockeys, he wanted to come to Lexington with me," Will explained. "We were able to talk business on the plane."

Her father said something about Jazz and his band,

but Melanie only half heard him. "Dad, can I borrow your cell phone?" she asked, reaching over the car seat again.

He handed it to her, and she dialed the barn phone again. Again no one answered. "Rats. Where could they be? Why don't they answer?"

"Why are you so worried?" Will asked.

"If Image doesn't settle down, she's going to be a wreck by the time her race comes around tomorrow. And she *has* to win," Melanie said emphatically. "Or Fredericka will have to sell her—to *Brad*. Which means I'd never get to see her, much less ride her." She dialed again, let it ring forever, and then sat back in frustration.

"*You* need to relax, Melanie, or you'll be a wreck by tomorrow," Will said. "We'll be there in ten minutes."

When they reached Turfway, Will slowed to turn into a parking spot. Flinging open the car door, Melanie jumped out. "See you at the barn," she called as she slammed the door.

She ran to the barn and to Image's stall. The top door was open, and Melanie leaned inside. Image was nosing around her straw. "Thank goodness you're all right!" Melanie gasped, opening the stall door and going inside. "I imagined all sorts of horrible things happening to you." The filly greeted her with a happy whicker, and Melanie gave her a relieved kiss.

"Of course she's all right," Ashleigh said. She and

Mike came over and stood in the doorway. "We kept her so busy, she didn't have time to fret. That's more than I can say for you." Ashleigh studied Melanie's face. "You still look pale. Did you get any sleep?"

"Three hours. Dad woke me up about one."

"Is Will here at the track?" Mike asked.

"Yeah. He had to park the car. He brought a client with him. A singer, I think."

"Did you have lunch?" Ashleigh continued to grill her. "You need to eat, Melanie. I don't want a repeat of your ride on Raven." Several weeks earlier Melanie had forgotten to eat and had passed out after racing Raven, one of Whitebrook's two-year-old fillies.

"Why don't we ask Will to take her for a late lunch?" Mike suggested. "It'll give them a chance to talk."

"No! I just got here. I need to stay with Image," Melanie insisted.

"Melanie, there's nothing to do," Ashleigh said.

"Image is fine," Mike agreed. "She's fit and ready for the race. If you keep hanging around, you're going to make her as nervous as you are."

Melanie's gaze shifted to Image, who was snuffling her jacket pockets. The filly did seem fine. "You're right. I *am* nervous. I just wish I had more time to get ready for tomorrow."

Ashleigh squeezed Melanie's shoulder. "You've

been doing the best you can, Melanie," she said reassuringly. "That's all you can do."

Melanie heard her dad's voice, and Ashleigh and Mike turned and waved.

"Why don't you spend some time with Image while we talk to your dad?" Mike said. "Last time he was in Lexington, we were in New York, so we didn't get to see him."

"Okay." When Ashleigh and Mike left, Melanie turned her attention back to Image. The filly had pulled a mouthful of hay from the net. She chewed it for a minute and then spit it out. Melanie frowned, wondering if Image had eaten anything since the previous night. She checked the grain tub, which was empty. But when she pushed aside the straw underneath the tub, she found more than half of Image's ration scattered and spilled on the floor.

Image *hadn't* been eating.

Had Mike and Ashleigh noticed? Melanie went to the stall door to call out to them. They were standing in a circle talking to Will, Jazz, Fredericka, and Vince Jones, who had just walked into the stable area. Melanie knew that Fredericka was concerned about Image winning the next day, too. Melanie wished she could reassure her that everything was fine.

Image stuck her nose under Melanie's arm. Then she banged the door with her hoof. When Melanie scolded her, the filly moved back to the hay net, grabbed a hunk in her teeth, and let it fall to the floor. Worried, Melanie laid her palm on the filly's chest. Image's heart was beating double time, and Melanie sucked in her breath.

She didn't care what Ashleigh and Mike thought. She knew the temperamental filly better than anyone. And she was sure of it—Image *wasn't* fine.

8

STEPPING BACK, MELANIE BIT HER LIP. SHE DIDN'T KNOW what else to do to make Image happier and more comfortable. If they were home, Melanie would turn her out in her pasture. That would have taken off her nervous edge. Here all she could do was walk her.

The stall door opened behind Melanie, and she turned just as Vince and Fredericka came in. "How's Image?" Vince asked.

"She's perfect!" Fredericka crooned as she held out a carrot. Image gobbled it eagerly, then nuzzled her owner for more.

Melanie hesitated. Should she tell them about Image not eating? Or would Vince think she was a worrywart, too?

"She's great, except . . ." Melanie hesitated.

Vince and Fredericka slanted their eyes in her direction. "Go on," Vince said impatiently.

When Melanie didn't say anything, he softened his tone. "Melanie, you've spent more time with this horse than all of us put together. If there's anything that's going to keep her out of the race tomorrow, you've got to tell me."

"She's not eating."

Fredericka sucked in her breath. "Well, that's not good!"

Vince only frowned.

"And she hates being here," Melanie added. "She may be a nervous wreck by tomorrow."

"Hold her head," Vince instructed.

Melanie grasped Image's halter, and Vince ran his hand down the filly's legs, then listened to her breathing.

"Her legs are cool and tight. Her lungs are clear and strong. I'd say the filly's ready to run." Crossing his arms, he eyed Melanie. "I know you and Fredericka are worried, and there's a lot at stake tomorrow," he said. "But I've been training horses for thirty years. And they've got personality differences, just like we do. A third of them don't eat before a race. A third of them develop nervous habits. The rest are just scared silly. Image's behavior isn't unusual." He pointed his finger at Melanie's chest. "You do your job tomorrow and this filly's going to win."

With those words, Vince left. Melanie made a face.

"Well, I guess that was Vince's idea of an uplifting speech," she said.

Fredericka laughed. "I think he was paying you a compliment. How very un-Vince-like."

Melanie shrugged. "I guess."

"Image seems edgy, but not more than usual. I'm going to leave you alone now, in case it's me that's exciting her," Fredericka said. "I'll see you soon, my princess." She fed Image another carrot, and then she left.

Melanie unhooked the feed tub. "Well, everyone else seems to think you're fine. Let's try some more grain."

She left the stall and walked along the aisle to the feed room. Will, Ashleigh, and Mike were still talking. Jazz stood beside Will, arms crossed, head cocked as if he was taking in every word. Dirt and straw clung to the hem of his long black coat.

Melanie went into the feed room, almost colliding with Dani, who was standing in the doorway. "Sorry," she said as she went over to the plastic feed barrels. "Did you get any sleep when you went home?" she asked the groom.

When Dani didn't answer, Melanie glanced over at her. She was hanging behind the doorjamb, peering outside. "What are you looking at?"

"Jazz Taylor," Dani whispered excitedly.

"Who?" Setting down the feed tub, Melanie came up beside Dani. She followed the other girl's gaze.

"Oh, him. He drove over with me and my dad."

Dani's eyes opened wide. "You drove in the same car with Jazz Taylor?"

"Uh, yeah." Melanie had no clue what the big deal was.

"And you didn't die?"

"No, I think I'm still alive."

"But he is so-o-o-o awesomely good-looking." Dani swooned against the doorjamb.

Melanie frowned. She had no idea why Dani, who was normally down-to-earth and practical, was acting like a crazed groupie.

"Do you think he'd give me an autograph?" Dani asked, clutching Melanie's arm.

"I guess. Why do you want it?"

"You don't know who he is!" Dani exclaimed.

"My dad mentioned he's a singer."

"Not just *any* singer. He's the lead singer of Pegasus, this incredible new band. Their single, 'Make My Day,' was number one all summer. I can't believe you never heard it."

Melanie shrugged. "Guess I've been too busy with Image."

"Will you ask him for an autograph for me?" Dani begged. "Please?"

"Dani, you can ask him yourself. He's just a person."

Dani made a face. "I couldn't."

"You could," Melanie said, giving her a push. Dani

stumbled out the door and into the aisle. Looking at Melanie over her shoulder, she hesitantly approached Jazz, who turned and smiled at her.

He did have a nice smile, Melanie noticed as she went back to the grain barrel. But maybe he just turned it on for his fans. Melanie turned her attention back to getting Image's grain.

She filled the tub with sweet feed and went back to Image's stall, shaking the grain and holding some out to Image in the palm of her hand. The filly ate the handful hungrily, and when Melanie hooked the tub to the wall, Image dove right in. Maybe Vince was right— Image was going to be fine.

A few minutes later Jazz came over and leaned on the stall door. "Is this Perfect Image?"

"Not quite so perfect today," Melanie said. "Did Dani get up enough nerve to ask you for your autograph?"

"Yeah, but I didn't have anything to write on, so I promised her a signed photo before I left."

"Gee, I'm surprised you don't carry photos in your pockets," Melanie said, sounding a little more obnoxious than she meant to.

"Ready for lunch?" Will asked as he joined them. "Ashleigh practically ordered me to feed you, Melanie." He nodded toward Image. "So how's the princess doing? I know you've been concerned, but she looks fine to me."

Melanie sighed. "I hope so. Well, let's go eat. How about the track kitchen?" she suggested as she opened the door of the stall. "It's cafeteria style, but the food's pretty good. And I don't want to be away from Image too long."

Will and Jazz agreed, and Melanie led the way to the backside cafeteria. As they walked past the different barns Melanie pointed out some of the top trainers and their horses. Jazz surprised her by knowing many of their names as well as the names of past winners they had trained.

"How do you know so much about horse racing?" she asked.

"My dad loved to bet on the ponies. He'd take me along for good luck."

"And were you?" Will asked.

He grinned. "Yeah, sometimes. I'd watch them parade around in the saddling paddock before the race. I could tell which one was too sore, which one was too doped up, which one was too scared, and which one was too stubborn."

Melanie snorted in disbelief. "Really?"

"How often did you pick winners?" Will asked. "I haven't been doing too well on my bets lately."

"About fifty-fifty. It was easy to tell which horse *wanted* to win," Jazz explained. "But—"

"How?" Melanie cut in, her tone skeptical. This

guy was pretty cocky if he thought he could pick the winner of every race.

"I could usually just tell. I know this sounds strange, but I just got good vibes from the winner."

They reached the track kitchen, and Melanie opened the door. She glanced skeptically at Jazz, not sure if he was joking or serious.

"Then why didn't you win every time?" Will asked, sounding pretty convinced.

Jazz shrugged. "You know how unpredictable racing is: problems in the gate, horses getting bumped, a bad jockey . . ."

Melanie winced. "Let's change the subject." Grabbing silverware and a tray, she walked over to the serving area. There were salads, desserts, and bowls of fruit lined up on the glass shelves. Behind the slanted glass partition were pans of steaming hot dishes. "Everything's home-cooked, but the burgers and fries are pretty greasy," she said.

Since it was past lunchtime, the cafeteria wasn't crowded. As they walked down the line Melanie noticed that people had stopped eating and were staring in their direction.

Even the food servers were whispering and giggling among themselves. Dani was obviously not the only one who thought Jazz was handsome.

"Excuse me, may I have a cheese omelet?" Melanie

asked the elderly woman behind the counter.

The server ignored her, her attention on Jazz. "You're Jazz Taylor, aren't you?" she asked, beaming like a little kid. "Oh, I'm so excited to serve you. The manicotti's delicious, you have got to try it."

"So much for my omelet." Melanie grabbed a fruit bowl and a cheese-and-tomato sandwich. Her father was piling lasagna, garlic breadsticks, a tossed salad, and chocolate cake onto his tray. "Susan has me on a low-fat diet," he explained. "I have to get the good stuff whenever I can."

Melanie found a table and sat down to eat. Jazz came over and set his tray next to hers. It was piled as high as her father's. "She kept giving me more food," he said, laughing.

They were almost finished eating when two girls came over with napkins. They wore matching jackets emblazoned with the name of a horse farm, so Melanie figured they were grooms.

"Are you, uh, um, J-Jazz Taylor?" one of the girls stuttered, her cheeks bright red.

"That's me." Jazz gave them his perfect smile.

"Oh," the other girl gasped. "We love your album. We love 'Make My Day.' We love you!"

"Give me a break," Melanie muttered. "Dad," she whispered, leaning over the table, "I'll meet you at the barn. I want to check on Image."

"Okay, Mel," Will said. "See you there."

Melanie dumped her tray and hurried from the cafeteria. She'd take Image for a long walk and try to think positive thoughts. Even if Image was fine, Melanie still had to ride her to a win. And one mistake by a jockey could win or lose a race. Should she hang back and assess what the other fillies were doing, or take the lead and go for it? It was only a six-furlong race, so she was better off starting in front and staying there.

Someone brushed past her, jarring Melanie out of her thoughts. She looked up, realizing that she was walking past the Townsend Acres barn. Brad was standing in the aisle, talking with one of his grooms. When she saw him, Melanie stopped. But before she could backtrack and duck around the corner of the building, Brad saw her.

"Melanie?" He waved her over. "Come here. I'd like to show you something."

Forcing a smile, Melanie walked over to him.

"I have a new horse," Brad said. He nodded to a groom. "Get Flashy Miss for me," he ordered.

"Why do you want to show *me* your new horse?" Melanie asked.

Brad chuckled, his attention on one of the stalls. "You'll find out."

The groom came out, leading a chestnut filly with a flaxen mane and tail. Melanie's eyes widened. The filly was gorgeous, with powerful hindquarters, a deep chest, and a long stride.

No wonder Brad was dying to show her Flashy Miss. He wanted to gloat.

"She's fantastic," Melanie said honestly.

"More than fantastic. She's a two-year-old out of Flash Dance, California's Colt of the Year in 1995. She's bred to win."

"Well, I'm sure she'll make a great addition to your string. You probably won't need to buy Image from Fredericka now," Melanie said, feeling a rush of relief.

Brad's chuckle was almost sinister. "You have no idea, do you, Melanie?"

"Idea of what?" Melanie asked warily.

"I can buy any horse I choose."

Melanie bristled. "You'll never own Image," she declared. "She's going to win tomorrow, and Fredericka won't need to sell her to you."

Brad inclined his head. "Oh, really? Obviously you haven't heard about the new entry in tomorrow's race." He gestured toward the chestnut filly. "Flashy Miss."

For a minute Melanie was too surprised to say anything. Finally she managed to say, "If she's got such great bloodlines, why would you enter her in such a low-profile race?"

Brad shrugged. "She's a maiden, just like Image. She's got to start somewhere. I can move her to a better grade of race anytime." A smile spread slowly across his face. "Besides, it's in my interest for Image to lose her race. So why not run Flashy Miss against her?"

Melanie's pulse raced, and she narrowed her eyes. "I don't care if Flashy Miss is the daughter of Seattle Slew. *Image is going to win*."

Brad laughed. "Think what you want, Melanie. But I paid good money for this filly. I don't expect her to lose."

Melanie didn't want to hear another word. Whirling, she ran down the aisle and around the corner of the barn. She didn't care how rich and powerful Brad was. She refused to let him intimidate her.

Fists clenched, she marched to Vince's barn. He was in his office, talking on the phone. Raising one finger, he signaled her to wait.

Melanie paced in front of his office door.

"We're shipping them to Florida tomorrow," Vince was saying.

At the end of the year many big trainers moved their horses south to warmer weather. Melanie knew Townsend Acres rented stalls at a Florida track. She couldn't believe Brad was so intent on beating Image that he'd keep Flashy Miss in Kentucky.

When Vince got off the phone, he gestured for her to come in.

"Why didn't you tell me Brad had entered a horse in our race?" Melanie asked him.

"I didn't think it mattered," Vince answered bluntly.

"Well, it does. He's got some new million-dollar filly running."

"So what?" Putting his hands behind his head, Vince leaned back in his desk chair.

Melanie couldn't believe he was being so thickheaded. "The only reason he entered her was to make sure Image doesn't win!"

"Your point?" Vince asked.

"My point is Brad is going to make it impossible for us to win tomorrow."

Vince's mouth tightened. "Do you want Image to win tomorrow?"

"Of course," Melanie said.

"Then go out there and do it," Vince said. "It shouldn't matter if you're racing against Secretariat. You still try your hardest and do your best. Flashy Miss may be a million-dollar horse, but that doesn't mean she's got the heart or the speed to beat Image."

"Right." Melanie flushed, suddenly feeling embarrassed. "Sorry."

"Don't be." The phone rang, Vince picked it up, and Melanie knew she was dismissed.

She hurried back to Whitebrook's barn, happy to see Dani, Ashleigh, and Mike there waiting for her, and for a minute she was tempted to tell them about Brad. But then she discarded the idea. Vince was right. Melanie couldn't let her anger get in the way. Image did have the heart and speed to beat any horse. That was enough.

She hurried back to Image's stall. She had a lot to

do that afternoon to get Image ready for the next day. Just like Brad, she was planning to win, too.

"No more pampering," Melanie told Image, dropping the soft brush in the grooming box. "I'm taking a break."

It was midnight. Image had been restless since dark. Joe and Melanie had taken turns walking her around the track and grazing her along the chain-link fence that circled the backside. Finally the filly had settled down long enough for Melanie to groom her and tempt her with a few bites of grain. Image was still alert, but Melanie felt as though she was about to drop.

With a weary sigh, Melanie blanketed the filly. Before leaving, she checked her water and hay net. Everything was fine.

"I'll be right back," she told the filly. "I'm sleeping in the stall with you, so don't mess it up."

Chilled to the bone, Melanie dragged herself to the heated tack room. Joe was stirring a mug of hot chocolate that he'd heated in the microwave.

"She's eating hay," Melanie said. "I think. Actually, I'm too tired to think."

Joe laughed. "You'll feel better after you drink this."

He handed her the mug, and she held it with both hands. "Thanks. This smells amazing."

Joe started for the door. "I'll check on her."

"No. You go home. Image and I will be fine, really."

"Okay. But you page me if anything happens or you need a break," Joe said. Melanie nodded, although she knew she wouldn't call him. Joe had a wife and two kids at home and didn't need to be bothered with Image after hours.

He left, and for a few minutes Melanie quietly sipped the warm drink. Then she put down the mug and unzipped her parka. This time she'd dressed for the weather. Hungry, she checked the tack room cupboard and found two granola bars. Her stomach growled at the sight of them. She'd turned down Will's offer of dinner at a four-star restaurant. She'd have time later for rich meals. That night Image was more important.

As she was unwrapping one of the granola bars she spotted Dani's CD player on the shelf. That afternoon Dani had played *Ground Zero*, Pegasus's album, while they'd cleaned tack. Melanie found the CD, stuck it in, and turned it on. "Make My Day" was the first song.

Make my day
Make my life
Make me happy
All my life.

Melanie listened to the tune and found she had to agree with Dani—the song Jazz had written was good.

Singing along with it, she brushed her teeth in the small sink and washed her hands. Then she turned off the CD and gathered her sleeping bag and parka. It was almost one in the morning. If she didn't get any sleep, she might as well forget about riding well the following day.

Steeling herself against the cold, she opened the door. The frigid air hit her like a snowball. Then she heard a loud crack, and she hurried down the dark aisle toward Image's stall.

"Stop it, Image," Melanie called.

Image greeted her with throaty nickers of joy.

"All right, you spoiled brat," Melanie said. She opened the stall door and went in, and the filly nuzzled her pockets eagerly. Melanie dropped the parka and sleeping bag in the corner and pulled the second granola bar from her pocket.

"Do you remember when I first met you?" she asked as she unwrapped the bar and broke off a piece. "You were locked in your stall, and I ate a granola bar and you smelled it on my fingers." She held out her palm, and Image gently lipped up a small piece of the bar. "I knew the minute I saw you that you were something special."

Tears welled in Melanie's eyes. "Oh, Image. I can't lose you. We've got to win tomorrow."

9

SATURDAY MORNING CAME TOO QUICKLY. MELANIE OPENED one eye, yawned, and decided she was still too tired to get up. Closing her eyes, she snuggled deeper into the sleeping bag. All night she'd tossed and turned, worrying about the race. She had no idea what time she'd finally fallen asleep.

A ray of sun hit her face, and Melanie rolled over to get away from it. Suddenly her eyes flew open.

A ray of sun! If the sun was up, then it was late. Pulling one arm from the sleeping bag, Melanie checked her watch. It was nine o'clock. She'd *never* slept this late on a race day.

She sat bolt upright. The stall doors were open, the sun was streaming in, and Image was gone.

Panicking, Melanie struggled to her feet, the sleeping bag still wrapped around her torso and legs. Where was Image? Had she forgotten to latch the doors?

She took a step, tripped on the sleeping bag, and fell flat on her face. Somebody laughed.

"Is this what you usually do on the morning of a big race?"

Melanie peered up at Jazz, who was standing in the open doorway.

"Where's Image?" she asked, trying not to sound too hysterical.

"Right out here."

"Is she all right?"

"Fine. Ashleigh is giving her a bath."

Melanie exhaled with relief.

"Image must have let you have the clean side of the bed. She has manure stains all over her," Jazz explained.

Melanie propped herself up on one elbow. "Ugh," she said. She'd fallen right into a pile herself. "Oh, boy. Christina's not going to be happy about her sleeping bag."

Awkwardly Melanie rolled onto her back, trying to squirm out of the bag, which was twisted around her legs.

"Need help?" Jazz asked, coming into the stall. He held out his hand. His black hair was pulled back in one braid. He was dressed in a forest green parka, faded blue jeans, and broken-in black leather boots.

"I need to hurry," Melanie said, taking his hand and kicking the sleeping bag away from her legs. "I've got to weigh in by eleven. Why didn't someone wake me up?"

"Actually, Christina did try to wake you, but you wouldn't budge. Joe told us you were up late last night with Image. Ashleigh decided to let you sleep."

"Morning, Mel," Christina greeted her cheerfully from the aisle. "We need to get over to the weigh-in room in two hours." Christina was riding both Dazzle and Rhapsody for Whitebrook. "Ready for breakfast?"

Melanie put her hand over the manure stain on the sleeping bag, trying to cover it up. "After I wash up and make sure Image is all right."

"Okay. I'll see you later, then." Christina looked from Jazz to Melanie with a silly grin on her face, and then left.

Melanie pulled a big clump of straw from her hair and glanced at Jazz. "Don't you have any autographs to sign?" she said brusquely. She didn't have time to worry about feeling awkward and ugly around some guy.

"Nope."

Melanie dragged the sleeping bag out of the stall and peeked down the aisle. Joe was holding on to Image while Ashleigh hosed her legs. Image pranced in a circle, kicking at the spray. On the other side of the aisle Christina was grooming Dazzle, and Dani was in Rhapsody's stall, trimming her whiskers. Melanie was obviously the only one who had overslept.

"Image really is beautiful," Jazz said. "I can see why you're so crazy about her."

Melanie sighed. "Right now I think I'm just crazy."

Jazz cocked his head quizzically, but Melanie didn't explain. "I've got to go," she said.

"Well, if I don't see you before the race, good luck," Jazz said.

"Thanks," Melanie said, dragging the sleeping bag down the aisle toward Image.

"Good morning, Sleeping Beauty," Ashleigh called.

Melanie rolled her eyes. "I don't think *beauty* is the word. How's Image? Do you need help?"

Ashleigh shook her head. "Not right now, but she'll need walking when I'm done. Mike won't be in until later, and Joe and I will have to pay some attention to Dazzle and Rhapsody, too."

"No problem. I'll go wash up and be back to help in one sec." Melanie carried the sleeping bag to the tack room and tossed it in a corner. She'd have to launder it later with the horse blankets. Grabbing her toiletry bag, she hurried to one of the backside shower rooms. On the way she met Vicky Frontiere, an experienced jockey and an old friend of Ashleigh's.

"Why aren't you riding down in Florida, where it's warm?" Melanie asked, following Vicky into the women's shower room.

"I have been. I've been flying back and forth between Florida and here. The Florida tracks aren't running today, so here I am. I get sunburned in Florida and frostbitten in Kentucky." She laughed.

Melanie set her toiletry bag on the shelf beside the sink. When she saw her reflection in the mirror, she grimaced. Her hair was flat on one side, where she'd slept on it. Dirt smudged her cheeks, and bits of straw were stuck all over her. No wonder Jazz had laughed at her. "I look terrible."

"Nah, you look like you slept with a horse," Vicky joked. "Hey, did you hear about Brad Townsend flying in Ricky Santiago to ride one of his new babies?"

"Ricky Santiago?" Melanie asked. "Isn't he the one who's earned over a million dollars in purse money this year?"

Vicky nodded. "Yeah. And Brad must be paying him a bundle, too. He's coming all the way from Texas for one little maiden race."

A chill ran up Melanie's spine. "Which race?" she asked, her voice hoarse.

"The third." Vicky bent to splash water on her face.

Melanie clutched the edge of the sink. That was her race. That meant Ricky Santiago was riding Flashy Miss!

Brad really was doing everything possible to make sure Image didn't win.

Melanie stared at the running water, her mind reeling. How could she and Image win now? She wondered if Vince knew. But Vince would only tell her that it shouldn't make a difference.

Melanie's face must have looked strange, because Vicky lowered her towel and asked, "Are you all right?"

"Yeah." Taking a deep breath, Melanie soaped her hands. "It's just that I'm riding in the third race, too."

"That's a bad break," Vicky said.

Melanie sighed. *You have no idea,* she thought miserably.

"Hey, if it isn't Melanie Graham," George Valdez, a jockey, called when Melanie and Christina came out of the women's locker room a couple of hours later. "I haven't seen you since you fell off that filly—*after* the race was over." Chuckling, George nudged Sammy Fingers, another jockey. "You remember that race, Sammy?"

"Pretty funny, George," Melanie retorted. She turned her back on them and sat on the couch facing the TV. Melanie was used to George and his snide remarks, but she was in no mood for kidding around with the other jockeys.

After walking and grooming Image, she'd eaten a light breakfast with Christina. Then the two girls had headed for the locker room. Melanie had showered and changed into green-and-purple silks, the colors of Tall Oaks. Christina wore blue and white, Whitebrook's colors. She was riding Dazzle in the second race and Rhapsody in the seventh.

The two girls had checked their weight allowances,

then weighed in with the clerk of scales. Now all they had to do was wait.

Snatching up a magazine, Melanie nervously leafed through the pages. Christina sat down next to her. Her cousin had been talking to Fred Anderson and Karen Groves, two other apprentice jockeys.

"Karen says Ricky Santiago's pretty high on himself," Christina said in a low voice. "And Fred says he's a real jerk."

"Like I care," Melanie grumbled, tossing the magazine aside.

Christina frowned. "Would you lighten up? It's just a race. You're going to be fine."

"I *can't* lighten up," Melanie retorted. "Don't you get it, Chris? If Image doesn't win, I'm going to *lose* her. If you knew you were going to lose Star, would you be able to lighten up?"

"No," Christina admitted, sounding dejected. "I'd be terrified. But you've got to think about winning the race, *not* losing Image."

"I know. That's what everyone keeps telling me," Melanie said miserably.

Christina squeezed Melanie's hand. "I'm sorry. I know the pressure stinks."

Melanie squeezed her cousin's hand back. "Thanks for listening, Chris."

The first race came on the TV, and Christina stood up. "I've got to get ready for my race. Will you be okay?"

Melanie nodded. "Dazzle looked great this morning. Good luck, cuz."

Christina hesitated. "Good luck, Mel," she said.

When Christina left, Melanie glanced around the jockeys' lounge, wondering where Ricky was. A hotshot jockey like Ricky would have a valet to care for his clothes and equipment, which meant he was probably soaking in the whirlpool and thinking about how good he and Flashy Miss would look in the win photo.

Leaning back against the sofa, Melanie closed her eyes and breathed deeply. *Inhale, exhale.* She visualized a perfect break from the gate and Image galloping across the finish line.

"Melanie, are you asleep?"

Melanie cracked open one eye. Karen Groves sat down next to her. She was a tiny blonde who'd been riding for a year and still hadn't won a race. "Was that Jazz Taylor I saw you with yesterday going into the cafeteria?"

Melanie closed her eyes once more and tried to concentrate on her breathing. "Yes, that was him." *Inhale, exhale.*

Karen let out such a shrill squeal of excitement that Melanie's eyes popped open once more. "I can't believe it!" she exclaimed. "Why didn't you say something? He is so majorly adorable!"

First he was amazingly good-looking, Melanie thought. *Now he's majorly adorable.* She seriously didn't care.

117

"What's he like? Is he nice? Does he have a girl-friend?" Karen demanded, clutching Melanie's arm.

Melanie pulled her arm away. "I didn't interview him, Karen. We just ate lunch."

"You ate lunch with him?"

Melanie had never seen Karen act this ditzy.

"Is he giving out autographs?" someone asked behind Melanie.

She looked over her shoulder. A half-dozen jockeys were hanging around the sofa, listening.

"He does," someone else answered. "Jelly and Jewel got him to sign their napkins."

Suddenly they were all talking and asking questions at once.

"I love his song."

"Was that him at the saddling paddock before the first race?"

"I have a poster of him at home. Do you think he'd sign it?"

Melanie wanted to scream. "Stop asking questions!" she yelled, jumping to her feet. "I don't know anything about the guy. I barely know him."

Melanie fled into the women's locker room and found a quiet spot on one of the benches. Sitting down, she stretched out her legs and leaned back against a locker. *Inhale, exhale.*

"Make my day. Make my life. Make me happy. All my liiiiife."

Melanie groaned. Someone was in the shower singing Jazz's song. She stuck her fingers in her ears.

Inhale, exhale. Melanie tried to visualize Image flying down the track. She tried to picture the filly pulling ahead of the other horses.

But all she could picture was Flashy Miss and Ricky Santiago streaking across the finish line.

Carrying her saddle, Melanie followed the other jockeys to the paddock for the third race. When she saw Image, she caught her breath. Mike was leading the filly around the oval, and he had his hands full. Image pranced beside him as if she were a queen in a parade. Head high, tail flowing, she gazed imperiously at the crowd as to say, *Look at me, everybody.*

And everybody was looking. Melanie could hear whispers as people read their programs to see who she was. As she walked toward the saddling stalls Melanie checked out the other fillies, who looked like typical two-year-olds—they hadn't grown into themselves, with slight builds, thin necks, or too-long legs. Her gaze went back to Image, who was trying to nip Mike's arm. When he shook the lead at her, she arched her neck and danced sideways, her powerful muscles rippling.

"That number four horse, Perfect Image, is beautiful," she heard one woman say.

Melanie grinned proudly.

"So is that chestnut filly that's just coming in," her

companion said. "The number two horse, Flashy Miss. Terrific breeding, too."

Melanie turned toward the gate and her grin faded. Flashy Miss was slightly smaller than Image but just as well built, and her expression was calmly determined.

"Melanie!" someone called from the crowd. Ashleigh, Cindy, and Fredericka were standing behind the railing. Fredericka waved a white handkerchief. Ashleigh yelled, "Good luck," and Cindy gave her a thumbs-up sign.

"How'd Christina and Dazzle do?" Melanie called.

Ashleigh held up three fingers. There had been twelve three-year-olds in the second race, so third was respectable.

Mike led Image into the saddling stall, and Melanie joined them. "Hello, you big show-off," she teased Image. Mike laughed. He wore a blue windbreaker with Whitebrook Farm written in white letters across the back. "We know what her next career will be after she retires from racing. She'll probably have her own TV show."

"At least she's not nervous," Melanie said, feeling nervous enough for both of them.

"We didn't give her time to be nervous," Mike said. "After you left for the weigh-in, we took turns entertaining her. Even Jazz."

"What did he do?"

"He sang her some new songs he's working on."

120

"That must have been amusing." Melanie ducked under Image's neck and helped Mike smooth the number four blanket and the saddle pad on the filly's back. Image fidgeted. "Hold still," Melanie scolded, although she knew exactly how Image felt.

When Mike put on the saddle, Melanie stepped out of the stall to see if she could spot Ricky Santiago. The jockey hadn't walked out with the rest of them.

"Too snobby to be seen with us," Jeremy King, a bug who was riding PayDay, the number six horse, had grumbled.

Then Melanie spotted Ricky, wearing red-and-black silks, the colors of Townsend Acres. He was lounging against the railing, talking to someone in the crowd. He didn't even look at Flashy Miss. Melanie peered over at the chestnut filly, who was in the number two stall. Brad stood beside her, arms crossed, watching the groom and handler saddle her. When he glanced Melanie's way, she ducked her head.

Mike was tightening the web girth. "So what's your strategy, Mel? I know this is an important race."

"No special strategy," Melanie admitted. Mike had always encouraged Melanie and Christina to use their instincts when riding in a race. "I'm going to see how Image acts. She might be a maniac or she might be quiet."

Mike chuckled. "I think you *do* have a strategy."

Melanie bit her lip. "I'm trying to stay calm, but"—

her voice dropped—"I'm scared to death," she admitted.

Just then Vince hurried up. "All right, Melanie. Here's my take on the field. Don't worry about the number one horse," he said, waving his hand in the filly's direction. "She'll tire out. The number three horse won't break clean, so you can beat her at the start." He shook his finger in her face. "That means no bucking coming out of the gate, right?"

Melanie gulped and nodded.

"The number five horse breaks to the left," Vince continued. "She's the one you'll have to watch out for."

"What about Flashy Miss?" Melanie asked.

Vince looked away, then shrugged. "Never seen her race," he said tersely.

He gave her a few more tips about the other horses, then left without even wishing her good luck. Melanie sighed, and Mike gave her shoulder a reassuring pat. "Melanie, I know you think the odds are stacked against you. But you're one of the finest young riders I know. All you can do is your best."

She tried to smile confidently. "I will. Image *deserves* the best."

Mike led Image from the stall for the second parade around the oval while a paddock judge inspected the horses and their equipment. Melanie pulled her whip from her boot and secured the strap on her helmet. She spied her father in the middle of a group of camera-clicking tourists. He waved, a big grin on his face, and hollered, "Good luck!" Jazz stood beside him, disguised with sunglasses and a Turfway baseball cap.

Melanie waved back. Then the paddock judge called, "Riders up!"

Turning, she hurried over to Image. Mike tried to hold the filly still, but Image pivoted away. Only when she paused to blink at the flash of a camera was Mike able to toss Melanie onto her back. Quickly she stuck her feet in the stirrups.

"This is it, kid," Mike said as he steered Image clockwise. Out of the corner of her eye Melanie saw Brad saunter over to the railing to talk with Fredericka. Melanie's pulse raced. What was he saying? Was he telling her all about Ricky and Flashy Miss? Was he telling her Image had no chance?

Then she realized what was going on. Brad wanted Melanie to see him. He wanted to shake her up.

It's not going to work. Melanie tore her gaze from them. Mike led Image to the gate, where the red-coated outrider waited to lead the horses for the post parade. Stopping, Mike unhooked the lead line and stepped back. "Good luck."

"Thanks, Uncle Mike." She grinned down at him, then steered Image out the gate behind the number three horse, Sky Racer. Just then she heard Fredericka's voice call out, "Good luck, my princess!"

Smiling, Melanie raised her whip in acknowledgment. Fredericka hadn't let Brad get to her.

"This is it," she whispered, scratching Image's withers. "It's just you and me now, girl. We're a team. A *winning* team. And remember . . ." She swallowed the lump rising in her throat. "Whatever happens, I'll always love you."

Image followed Sky Racer, a bay filly, onto the track, where the pony riders picked them up. The six horses paraded clockwise up the track in front of the grandstand. The air was brisk but the sun was warm, and the crowd had gathered outside along the railing. The band played "Kentucky Woman" by Neil Diamond. Image rolled her eyes and shied away from the noise and confusion.

"Don't get too close," Melanie warned the pony girl, who jogged alongside on her chunky palomino. "She might kick. Could you ride between us and the grandstand?"

"No problem," the other girl said, swerving her horse to the left. Image bobbed her head nervously.

Melanie began to hum "Make My Day" to calm her.

The filly flicked her ears and began to jig. Melanie bounced lightly on the vinyl saddle. *Inhale, exhale.* She checked out the tote board. The odds on Flashy Miss were two to one. Image's odds were five to three. The bettors must have liked Flashy Miss's breeding, but they also liked Image's workout time.

When the horses passed the grandstand, Melanie

squeezed Image into a warm-up canter. The filly felt smooth and fluid. They cantered past Flashy Miss. Ricky was balanced in the stirrups, a frown on his face.

Just then Melanie realized that Ricky had never ridden Flashy Miss before. *That* would be her advantage!

She felt a rush of confidence. She knew Image's every mood and move. She'd always told herself that one day all her attention to Image would pay off. Maybe this would be the day.

Melanie perched in the stirrups. The brisk wind buffeted her cheeks. For the first time since Brad's announcement, she felt hopeful.

When they reached the starting gate, Melanie kept Image away from the other horses. As she circled her, she kept on humming Jazz's song. The number one horse, Whisper, balked before loading. The gate crew linked hands behind her rump and pushed her in, slamming the doors. Flashy Miss walked in like a pro. Sky Racer reared, almost knocking over the assistant starter, but finally she lunged forward and into the chute.

Image was next. Melanie's stomach tightened. Steering Image out of her circle, she pointed her toward the number four stall. The filly stopped dead. The assistant starter came up to grab her bridle.

"Give her a second," Melanie said. He must have recognized them from the day they were approved, because he backed off.

White-eyed, Image stared at the chute. "You're okay," Melanie crooned. "It's the same as the one at Whitebrook." Melanie touched her with her heels. Neck arched, Image walked stiff-legged into the padded stall, and Melanie let out a sigh of relief.

The gate clanged, and they both jumped. "Just pretend you're at Whitebrook," Melanie said, trying to calm her own jittery nerves. While they waited for the rest to load, Melanie took her mind off her butterflies by checking out the other horses and repeating Vince's assessment of each.

She glanced at the two horses loading on her right. PayDay would break sloppily. Belle's Song would lug left. She glanced at the three horses on her right. Whisper would sprint to the front and tire out. Sky Rider might rear in the stall. Melanie wished she knew what Flashy Miss would do.

Melanie turned her attention back to Belle's Song, the horse next to her. If the gray filly lugged left, Melanie would have to stay out of her way—

Suddenly a loud clang startled Melanie, and her eyes swung left again. Sky Racer had reared back on her haunches. An assistant starter climbed into the chute to hold the filly's bridle. Melanie knew Linda Simms, the jockey riding her. Linda had both hands locked onto the horse's mane, and she looked terrified.

"It's post time!" the announcer hollered across the track. A hush fell over the starting gate. Melanie tensed. She wound a hunk of mane around her fingers. Image danced beneath her. The starting bell rang. The doors flew open.

"They're off!"

Image leaped from the stall as if she were airborne. Melanie held tight to the mane, trying not to get left behind. The filly lunged awkwardly, almost bumping into Belle's Star, who had leaped into her path. On their left, Melanie could see Ricky Santiago expertly pilot Flashy Miss from the number two gate. In three strides the chestnut filly had streaked ahead and was galloping on the rail before the other fillies had gotten their legs under them.

Tugging on Image's right rein, Melanie got her away from Belle's Star and into the space left by Flashy Miss. Whisper was galloping along the rail behind Flashy Miss. Melanie had no idea what had happened to Sky Rider. Setting her fists on Image's neck, she balanced lightly over her withers. The filly was running with long, controlled strides. So far so good.

They galloped past the second pole. Four furlongs to go. Melanie glanced to her right. Belle's Song and PayDay were running neck and neck about a half length behind her. On her left Whisper still hugged the rail behind Flashy Miss. Melanie had only wide-open space in front of her.

"Okay, Image. You've got the speed," she told the filly. "Use it."

Image flicked her ears, as if making sure she'd heard Melanie right. Then she lengthened her stride. Slowly, easily, she pulled farther ahead of PayDay and Belle's Song. On the rail, Whisper was already tiring. The only competition left was Flashy Miss. In a six-furlong race, Melanie had no time to wait. If they were going to catch her, she had to make her move.

Melanie eyed Brad's blue-blooded filly. As they rounded the far turn to the homestretch, Ricky still had her rated. But her nostrils flared pink. Her mouth frothed.

Image wasn't even breathing hard.

Melanie narrowed her eyes. "Go, princess. Do it for Fredericka and me. Show the world how fast you are."

Flattening her ears against her head, Image poured it on. Melanie felt the power radiate from her in waves of energy, and her heart pounded in time to the filly's ground-eating strides.

One stride, two strides, and they pulled alongside Flashy Miss. Ricky glanced their way, his gaze hard behind the lenses of his goggles. He waved his whip along his mount's neck.

Three strides, four strides. Image blew past them. Melanie heard the whack of Ricky's whip as it rose and fell against Flashy Miss's flanks.

Two furlongs to go. Melanie could see the eighth pole. There was no way the other horses could catch up. There was no way they'd beat Image to the finish line.

The filly was faster than any horse Melanie had ever ridden. She felt a whoop of joy rise in her throat. She wanted to wave her whip in the air and shout with happiness.

Image was going to win!

Suddenly Image threw up her head and skidded to a halt, her hocks digging into the ground as if she were a reining horse. Melanie flew onto the filly's neck. Her feet flopped from the stirrups, and her hands clung desperately to Image's mane.

Image spun and reared, her forelegs raking the air. Melanie locked her arms around the filly's neck. The reins flapped uselessly.

The filly landed, pawed the footing, and bellowed a challenge to the oncoming horses. Melanie pulled herself back into the saddle. She yanked off her goggles and gasped.

Image had spun completely around and was facing the oncoming field of horses, which was galloping straight for them!

10

Melanie stifled a scream of terror.

The other jockeys were too busy battling it out for second place to notice that the leader had stopped running. Even if they did see Image, they were moving with such speed that there was no time for them to stop or swerve.

Image reared again and let out a furious call. Melanie knew she had to do something fast or the other horses would crash into them. In a split second she saw her chance. Whisper and Flashy Miss were still on the rail. PayDay and Belle's Star were neck and neck about five feet away from them. That left a narrow gap between the two pairs of running horses.

Snatching up her reins, Melanie took a strong hold on Image's mouth. The filly shook her head, resisting.

"No!" Melanie shouted angrily, trying to get Image's attention away from the horses. Then she clamped her legs against the filly's sides, aimed her at the space between the four horses, and hit her hard with the whip.

Startled, Image leaped forward into the hole, and the galloping horses surged safely around her. A furious Image yanked the reins from Melanie's sweat-slick fingers, wheeled, and took off after them, darting back through the gap she'd just gone through, except this time she was running in the right direction. She passed the leader, Flashy Miss, a length before the finish line.

They'd won.

Melanie was too exhausted to even notice. Legs hanging, she let Image canter around the clubhouse turn. An outrider drew up alongside them.

"You all right?" he called.

Weakly Melanie nodded.

Steering his horse next to Image, he grabbed the right rein. "That was quite a ride out there." Melanie nodded again. Her fingers were sore. Her shoulders ached. Her legs felt wooden.

The outrider snubbed Image's head close to his thigh and forced her to turn back toward the clubhouse. Melanie glanced at the tote board. Image's name and number were first. Flashy Miss second. Pay-Day third. Melanie knew the results would quickly change. Image might have won, but the stewards would never let her keep the win.

Almost immediately Image's name dropped to last, and Flashy Miss rose to number one. But Melanie didn't care about winning first place or about the purse money. She didn't care about being in the winner's circle. Truth be told, Image had beaten Ricky Santiago and Flashy Miss. With her usual flair for the dramatic, she'd proven that *she* was the fastest horse. Surely that was all that mattered.

"Too bad," the outrider said. "The crowd was rooting for you."

Tears filled Melanie's eyes. Dropping onto Image's neck, she hugged the filly. "It's all right, girl. We still did it," she whispered. Image had showed Fredericka and the rest of the racing world that she had the speed to be a winner, if she could just follow the rules.

When they reached the gate leading into the backside, Melanie dismounted. Her legs wobbled, and she leaned against the filly's ribs. Mike walked up, his face a blank, a blue-and-white cooler slung over his arm. He snapped the lead to the bit and thanked the outrider.

Without a word he unbuckled the girth and slid off the saddle. With one hand he covered Image with the cooler. Then he ran his other hand down each of her legs. "Her tendons are still cool and tight," he remarked, as if Melanie were just another jockey and Image were just another horse.

Finally Melanie couldn't stand it any longer. "Aren't you going to say anything?"

He cracked a wide smile. "Wildest race I ever saw."

Melanie pulled off her helmet. Her hair was soaked with sweat. Bending at the waist, she took deep breaths. She felt light-headed with relief—not only because of Image's speed, but because no one had gotten hurt. It was a miracle.

"I think that race will go down in Turfway history," Mike added with a chuckle. "Some reporter will call you Wrong Way Graham, and you'll be famous forever."

Melanie groaned. "Just how I want to be remembered."

She straightened up, the blood rushing to her feet. She grabbed on to Mike's arm, steadying herself.

"Okay?" he asked, and she nodded. "I'll be fine once I talk to Fredericka. Once she tells me how awesome Image is and that she'd never sell her." She glanced around. "Do you know where she and Vince are?"

Mike shook his head. "Fredericka usually watches from her box in the grandstand. I know that's where Will and Jazz went."

Taking the saddle, Melanie followed Mike toward the backside. Ashleigh and Cindy were waiting for them, along with several reporters. Unlike Mike, they had no problem bombarding her with questions.

"What happened out there?"

"Why did your horse turn around?"

"Will there be an inquiry?"

Melanie stopped, speechless. Reporters often mobbed Christina and Ashleigh, but this was a first for her.

"Excuse me." Ashleigh pushed her way through the reporters. "Ms. Graham has no comments." Putting her arm around Melanie, she steered her through the gate after Mike and Image.

"Can't blame the kid," one reporter said, chuckling. "Hey, there's Brad Townsend. I'd like to get a few words from him."

Cindy came over and gave Melanie an unexpected hug. "And I thought I had seen it all!" she said, laughing.

Melanie rolled her eyes. "It was my fault. I got too confident. I lost my concentration too early, and . . ." She stopped when she noticed Cindy was grinning at her.

"What?"

"Ashleigh and I clocked her," Cindy said in a low voice. "Even with her crazy stunt, she almost broke the track record for six furlongs."

Melanie was stunned. She knew Image had been fast. Now she knew *how* fast.

"Wow! Wait until I tell Fredericka. She'll be so excited."

Ashleigh frowned. "Melanie, it does prove Image is fast; but as you discovered today, it takes more than speed to win a race. She's got to behave herself, too.

There's probably going to be an official inquiry."

Melanie ignored her aunt's reservations. "This was Image's first race. She'll do better next time. All we needed to do was prove that Image has what it takes. Almost breaking the track record should be enough to persuade them. Besides, look at her!" Smiling excitedly, she turned to Mike and Image. The filly was twirling in a circle, still champing on the bit. "Mike said her legs were cool, and she isn't even winded."

Ashleigh looked unconvinced, but Melanie didn't care. She grabbed Cindy's arm. "Where is Fredericka? I've got to talk to her before I burst."

"She was in the grandstand with your father and Jazz."

"Will you find her for me? Please? I've got to talk to her."

Cindy nodded, and Melanie gave Image one last pat. "I'll be back to help cool you out as soon as I can," she told the filly.

Melanie watched with pride as Mike led Image away, then she headed back to the jockeys' lounge.

"Great trick riding, Graham," someone said as she passed by. It was one of Vince's grooms.

"Yeah, thanks," Melanie muttered. Where was Vince, anyway? She knew he'd have plenty to say about Image's crazy race. *Everyone* would.

When Melanie reached the jockeys' lounge, she paused outside the door. Her legs were still wobbly, and the saddle felt as if it weighed a ton. She started to open the door, steeling herself for the onslaught of jeers from the other jockeys. *Image almost broke the track record*, she reminded herself. *That's nothing to be ashamed of.*

An hour later Melanie hurried into the grandstand. Cindy had reported that Fredericka was still there with Will, Jazz, Beth, and Ian. Melanie spotted her father in Fredericka's box, but she didn't see Fredericka anywhere.

When Melanie came down the stairs to the box, her father clutched dramatically at his chest. "You almost gave me a heart attack!" he exclaimed.

Melanie laughed and hugged him. "You'd better start getting used to it, Dad."

She looked around again for Fredericka, spotting Brad and Lavinia at the bar with a noisy group of people. Celebrating, no doubt. But Melanie didn't care that Flashy Miss had officially beaten Image. Everyone who had been watching knew who was the faster horse.

A loud laugh caught her attention. Jazz was standing in front of the viewing glass overlooking the racetrack, the daughters of the racetrack officials and big-shot horse owners surrounding him. As usual, they were all wearing the latest outfits, makeup, and hairstyles.

Melanie touched her own hair, still damp from the shower. She'd thrown on clean barn clothes and finger-combed her hair. She hadn't had time for makeup. She was sure she looked terrible.

Melanie tore her gaze away. "Do you have any idea where Fredericka is?" she asked her father.

"She and Vince went off together a little while ago, but I'm not sure where."

"Oh, no." Melanie winced. "Ashleigh said there might be an official inquiry. I bet the stewards will want to talk to me, too."

"You? But you handled her so well. Thanks to you, no one got hurt," Will argued.

"Yes, but the stewards have to be sure there was no foul play. It's okay, Dad. I'm not worried. They already bounced Image to last. What more could they do?" Melanie said.

Plenty, she suddenly realized.

She'd been so excited after the race, she hadn't really thought about the consequences of an inquiry. Now she was so nervous, she chewed a fingernail. Her stomach felt hollow, but she was too wound up to eat.

Turning, Melanie scanned the doorway leading into the grandstand. Her heart skipped a beat when she saw Vince enter with Fredericka. Vince's expression was surly, as usual, but Fredericka looked crestfallen. Something was wrong.

"Oh, no. I've got to find out what happened," Melanie told her father.

"I'm coming with you."

Melanie took the stairs two at a time.

"What did the stewards say?" Melanie asked, not wasting any time.

Taking her elbow, Vince led her back through the doorway into a quiet corner of the hall. Will followed with Fredericka.

"The stewards didn't blame you, Melanie," Vince explained. "So you don't need to worry about suspension. However . . ."

Melanie gulped nervously.

"They've suspended Image from the track for two weeks."

"Okay, I can handle that," Melanie said, relieved it wasn't worse. "Obviously she needs more training before she races again. We would've given her at least two weeks off before her next race, anyway." She glanced at Fredericka. The older woman was looking down at her hands, as if unable to meet Melanie's eyes.

"There's more," Vince said, almost gently. "After Image's embarrassing performance today, Fredericka has decided to sell her."

"Embarrassing? What?" Melanie felt as if someone had hit her in the face. "But Fredericka, you can't sell her. Didn't Cindy tell you? Image almost broke the track record! She's got the speed and the heart to do anything—you've got to believe me."

"Melanie." Vince cut her off, his voice firm. "Fredericka did not make this decision lightly. It's not just the race. It's Image's difficult behavior on and off the track. She's more trouble to Fredericka right now than she's worth. You had to sleep in the barn with her for the past two nights, for Pete's sake. How long can that go on? And then today's race—she could've killed you."

"I know, I know, but she didn't. All Image needs is patience," Melanie began, but when she saw the look on Fredericka's face, her protests died and her eyes filled with tears. There was no use arguing. She could see it in the older woman's expression. Fredericka had given up on Image.

"Well, well, just the people I need to talk to," Brad Townsend said, sidling between Melanie and Will. "Fredericka, Lavinia and I would love to take you to dinner. I believe we have an important deal to discuss?"

Melanie ducked her head, refusing to let Brad see her tears. She couldn't believe how despicable he was, barging in with his ingratiating smile when he knew exactly what they were discussing.

"Excuse me," Melanie said. Turning, she walked away with her head high. But when she went out the exit doors, her whole body collapsed, and she dropped down on the steps, sobbing with despair and exhaustion.

"Melanie! What's going on?" Cindy called when

139

she saw Melanie. She hurried up the steps. "What happened?"

Melanie choked on her tears. How could she explain to Cindy that her heart was broken? Every day racehorses were bought, sold, ruined, and retired. Jockeys weren't supposed to fall in love with the horses they raced.

"I'm just really tired," she lied. Wiping her eyes, Melanie stood up.

Cindy frowned worriedly. "Did you find Fredericka?"

Melanie shook her head. "I'm sorry, I can't talk. I've got to get back to Image." And without another word of explanation, she ran down the stairs and pushed her way through the double doors.

She reached the Whitebrook stalls, breathing a sigh of relief when she saw that no one was around but Dani, who was walking Image, quietly humming to herself.

"Where is everybody?" Melanie asked. Her tears had dried and she'd stopped at the backside rest room to wash her face. She didn't want to telegraph her sorrow to the world.

"At the saddling paddock. Christina and Rhapsody are about to race."

"Oh, right." Melanie had forgotten all about them. "I'll take Image. Why don't you go and watch?"

"Hey, thanks," Dani said. "By the way, that was a

great race. You guys should have won anyway. Image was awesome."

"Yeah, well . . ." Melanie's lower lip trembled, and she stopped herself before she broke down once more.

Dani handed her the lead line. "She's almost all cooled out."

"Thanks for everything, and wish Christina good luck for me," Melanie called as Dani hurried off.

She led Image out of the barn and away from the busy backside, looking for a quiet place to hide. Soon the filly was grazing happily along the chain-link fence that circled Turfway's property. Melanie couldn't believe that only an hour earlier she'd been on cloud nine. Image's fast time had lulled her into thinking the filly was safe from Brad. Now, even after all her hard work and sleepless nights, everything she'd worried about for the past few months was coming true. Brad and Fredericka would probably finalize their deal over dinner, and Image would be shipped directly to Townsend Acres from Turfway. Melanie would never see her again.

Oblivious to her future, Image moved from clump to clump of grass, cropping hungrily. Melanie buried her face in her mane and cried, stroking the filly's muscled shoulder over and over. Image was everything she'd always wanted. She couldn't stand to lose her.

"Melanie?"

Melanie glanced over her shoulder. Jazz was standing on the other side of the fence, his fingers folded over the metal links.

"We've been looking all over for you," he said.

"Why? Is something wrong?" Melanie said, wiping her nose.

"No, your dad was just worried when you ran off," Jazz explained.

She looked away. "Tell him I'm fine. I'll meet him back at the barn."

"Okay," Jazz said, and walked slowly off with his hands in his pockets.

The sun was beginning to set when Melanie finally led Image back to the Whitebrook stalls. The van was parked by the side of the barn, and Joe was putting wraps on Pirate. Melanie had thought she was too drained and numb to feel anything anymore. But when she saw Pirate getting ready to go home without Image, her heart grew heavy, and new tears sprang into her eyes.

Her father was sitting on the chair by Image's stall door. When he spotted her, he jumped up. His brow was furrowed, and he quickly strode over to give her a hug. "Are you all right? I got worried when it started to get dark."

Melanie nodded. "I'm fine, Dad. But please, don't make me talk about it."

"We're going to load up in ten minutes," someone

said behind her. "Better get that black filly wrapped up."

Melanie grew rigid. She glanced over her shoulder, expecting to see Brad, but it was Joe.

"Image isn't going back to Whitebrook, Joe," she explained, her voice cracking.

Joe frowned and gave Will a questioning look. Will smiled at his daughter. "Joe's right, Melanie. Image *is* going back to Whitebrook tonight—and forever."

Melanie shook her head in confusion. "What are you talking about?"

"*I* bought Image," Will explained, his smile widening. "At least, Graham Productions bought Image. The company's been doing well, and Susan and I have been looking for an investment. A Thoroughbred wasn't exactly what we had in mind," he added with a chuckle. "But I figure I'm not just making a business investment. I'm making an investment in my daughter's future."

Melanie opened and shut her mouth, completely speechless. Was she dreaming?

"Image is yours, Melanie," Will said softly. "To race, to train, to turn into a champion—and to love forever."

11

MELANIE WAS TOO STUNNED TO SPEAK. HAD SHE HEARD her father right? He had bought Image?

"Are—are you joking?" she stammered, still not willing to believe it.

Will put his arm around her. "I'd never joke about something so important."

Only then did Melanie realize her father was serious.

"You mean she's really mine?" Whirling, she flung her arms around Image's neck. "You're mine! Finally mine!"

Startled, the filly jerked her head up, pulling the lead line from Melanie's grasp. Melanie gasped, remembering all the times Image had bolted free. But the filly only ambled into her stall, looking for her dinner. Melanie shut the door, then turned to face her father. Tears blurred

144

her eyes, and she was smiling so hard her cheeks hurt.

"Do you know what this means?" Melanie said giddily. "No more worrying about Image being sold! No more fears about losing her!" Dizzy with happiness, she swayed against her father. He caught her and steered her to the chair by the door.

Plopping into it, she began to laugh uncontrollably. She bent over and pressed her hand against her stomach, trying to stop. Finally she gave one last hiccup and straightened up.

Jazz came up behind Will and regarded Melanie curiously.

"Does she do this often?" he asked.

"Only when there's a full moon," Will replied.

Joe came over again. "Is Image ready to go home now?" he asked, smiling.

"Yes!" Melanie exclaimed eagerly. "Let's get her back to Whitebrook before anyone changes their mind or something horrible happens. Let me get her shipping wraps."

She hurried to the tack room, threw open the door, danced inside, and let out a whoop. Raising her arms high, she twirled and gyrated across the floor to the supply trunk. Someone whistled and clapped, then called, "Bravo, bravo." It was Jazz.

He leaned against the doorway. "Joe said to hurry. Pirate's already loaded."

"Be right there." Bending, Melanie rooted through

145

the trunk and pulled out four fuzzy wraps. She threw two to Jazz, and he caught them easily.

Joe had led Image from the stall and hooked her into crossties. Quickly Melanie put the wraps on her legs and led her up the ramp and into the van. She kept glancing over her shoulder, worried that any minute Brad would appear to tell her it was all a mistake. It would take her a while to get used to the idea that Brad was no longer a threat.

Image touched Pirate's nose in greeting, and Melanie backed her into the stall beside him. After snapping the chains to the halter rings, she stepped back. She couldn't take her eyes off the filly. *Her* filly.

"Joe, I know it's not allowed, but can I ride back here with the horses? Just this once?" Melanie pleaded, her hands clasped in front of her. "I can sit on a bale of straw. There's plenty of room. Pirate rides quietly, and Image . . . she knows she's going home. She'll be fine."

Joe hesitated.

"If something happens, I'll take full responsibility," Will said.

Joe opened his mouth.

"Oh, thank you, Joe!" Melanie blurted before he could say no.

Jazz carried a bale of straw up the ramp and set it against the wall in front of the stalls.

"And thank you," Melanie told Jazz as she started to sit down.

"Hey, that's mine. Get your own bale," Jazz said.

"You're riding in the van, too?"

"Sure beats a limo." Sitting down, he stretched out his long legs.

Joe brought up another bale and placed it end to end with the one Jazz was sitting on. Melanie sat down, wondering why in the world Jazz would want to ride in a smelly horse van.

"I'll follow you guys in my car," Will said from outside. "I think we should have a celebration dinner. I'll call Mike and Ashleigh on the cell phone and make a reservation."

He was still talking when Joe raised the ramp. For a second it was pitch black inside. Melanie blinked, waiting for her eyes to adjust. A faint light shone through the two side windows, and she was able to see the outline of Image's head. The filly was contentedly munching hay from the net hanging between her and Pirate.

Sighing, Melanie leaned back against the wall and shut her eyes. The motor roared to life, vibrating the wall and floorboards, and the van pulled slowly away. Only when the van reached the highway did Melanie completely relax. Even then she pinched herself just to make sure it wasn't a dream.

"Feeling better?" Jazz asked.

Melanie looked over at him. She could see his silhouette in the dim light. He was slouched against the wall, a hay stalk between his lips.

"I've never felt this good in my whole life."

He chuckled. "Even I was excited when your father told me what he'd done."

"I feel like the luckiest girl in the world," Melanie said, smiling dreamily. "So, how did you like your first day at Turfway?" she asked.

"I loved it."

Melanie laughed. "And now you're topping off the experience with a ride in a stinky old horse van."

"Suits me fine. You're not the only one who needs to hide once in a while."

Melanie snorted. "Oh, right, like your life is so tough."

When he didn't say anything, Melanie knew he was serious. "Sorry. I don't really know you, so I shouldn't make any judgments. I guess even rock stars have problems."

He looked away, and Melanie wanted to kick herself. Even she could hear the sarcastic tone on her voice. "I didn't mean it that way. It's just hard to believe that someone who's more famous than I could ever dream of could be unhappy."

"Well, this wasn't exactly my dream," Jazz finally said. "My dream was to write great songs."

"What happened?"

"A year ago I made a demo tape of 'Make My Day.' For months I made the rounds, trying to get someone to listen to it. Finally a small record producer let me audition. He decided that he didn't just want my song, he wanted me. He said I had star appeal. Since then I haven't had time to write. All I do is sing at shopping malls and on talk shows."

"Why don't you tell him you don't want to do it anymore?" Melanie asked.

"My contract. I was so excited about finally getting the chance to sing the song that I didn't read the fine print. That's why I've been talking with your dad. My contract's up at the end of the month. I'm pretty sure I want to sign with Graham Productions."

"My dad's the greatest."

"No doubt."

Melanie giggled. "He was even the greatest *before* he bought Image."

"I agree. Will feels I should have more time to write, too, as well as more creative control. He says we should be able to strike a balance between writing, performing, and promoting."

Melanie smiled. "Good old Dad."

"So tell me more about Image," Jazz urged, changing the subject. "When did you first start working with her?"

Melanie was more than happy to fill Jazz in. She told him about Image crashing Fredericka's tea party. "And I mean *crashing*," Melanie said. "We picked up broken china and glass for hours."

"But you never gave up on her."

"I almost gave up many times. Then Christina or

Ashleigh or Kevin would remind me why I needed to have faith and be patient."

"Why?"

"Because I believed in her—and because I loved her." Emotion rose in Melanie's throat, and she had to look away.

For the rest of the ride Melanie and Jazz sat in silence. Melanie closed her eyes, suddenly exhausted. She'd been under so much strain, but now the worrying was over.

When Melanie felt the van slow down, she opened her eyes and jumped up, peering out the window. "We're here," she told Jazz as they turned into Whitebrook's driveway. He stood and peered out the window, too.

"It's beautiful," he said. "I'd love a tour sometime."

The van pulled up to the barn, and the ramp was lowered. Kevin, Dani, Cindy, and Ian grinned up at her.

"Welcome home, Image!" they cheered in unison. "Congratulations, Mel!"

Melanie laughed. "Thanks, guys."

Kevin came up the ramp with two lead lines. He was smiling from ear to ear. "Ashleigh and Mike told us the news as soon as they got here with Dazzle and Rhapsody."

"How'd Christina do?" Melanie asked. "Where is she?"

"Inside taking a shower. She placed third out of a field of twelve on Dazzle. She got boxed in, and Dazzle just didn't have the acceleration to get out. Rhapsody came in fourth—" He was about to describe what had happened next when Image butted him with her nose.

"Hey, wait your turn," Kevin said.

"I bet she's dying to go out in her pasture," Melanie said. She snapped the lead to Image's halter ring and unhooked the chains. "She's had enough of those cramped stalls at the track."

"Cramped? If you recall, I spent a whole afternoon making Image a double stall," Kevin retorted. "Next time she'll be demanding her own barn."

Melanie led Image down the ramp, with Kevin and Pirate right behind her. Jazz was talking to Dani, who stared up at him, awestruck.

Will had just driven up and was getting out of his rental car. "Celebration at the Paddock Club in one hour!" he announced. "Everybody's invited."

"One hour," Melanie groaned. "That doesn't give me much time to soak in a hot tub."

Bending over, she took off Image's wraps, which wasn't easy, since she had to avoid the excited filly's prancing hooves. Finally she got them off, and Dani brought over Image's turnout rug.

"Sorry to make you tear yourself away from Jazz," Melanie teased.

Dani turned red. "He's really nice," she whispered. "He had his agent FedEx a picture of the band to his hotel. And he's autographing it for me!"

Melanie shook her head. Jazz was just a guy; she didn't understand why Dani acted so giddy around him.

Finally Image was ready to be turned out. When Melanie led her through the gate and took off her halter, Image raced across the pasture, bucking and squealing. Only when she settled into a high-stepping trot did Kevin lead Pirate in to join her. The two cantered up the hill, disappearing over the dark horizon, and then circled and trotted back. Stars sparkled overhead, and the moon peeped from behind a cloud. Finally the horses began to crop the frosty grass.

Melanie leaned on the top board of the fence and sighed with pleasure. "I never thought this day would come," she told Kevin. "I always wished Image was mine. But I never dreamed she ever would be."

"Hey, you deserve her," Kevin said.

"I'd like to make a toast," Will said an hour later.

After they'd gotten home, everybody had quickly showered and changed. Melanie had taken a few minutes to find a decent outfit, blow-dry her hair, and dash on some makeup. She'd driven over with Dani, Cindy, Christina, Parker, and Kevin—all packed into one car. Ashleigh and Mike had ridden with Beth and Ian. Will and Jazz had driven from their hotel. Now everybody was seated around a table in the private room of the Paddock Club.

"Actually, I'd like to make several toasts," Will amended as he raised his wineglass. "To Ashleigh and Mike, who have been wonderful friends and terrific role models for my daughter. To Christina, who ran two great races—in the right direction!"

Melanie rolled her eyes, and everybody laughed.

"To Ian and Kevin, who helped train Image," Will continued. "And to Melanie, my daughter"—with a serious expression, he looked down at Melanie, who sat on his right—"who has taught me more about patience and faith than she knows."

Embarrassed, Melanie looked away and took a sip of her water.

"And last but not least, to Perfect Image, racehorse extraordinaire, co-owned by Graham Productions and Jazz Enterprises, and soon to be a champion!"

Jazz Enterprises! Melanie choked on her water. She bent over, coughing, and Christina whacked her on the back.

"Jazz is in on this?" Melanie gasped. But no one was paying attention to her. Everybody was clinking glasses and congratulating each other.

Image wasn't her horse at all! Why hadn't her father told her? She knew Will had bought the filly as a business investment—but to Melanie it felt as though he'd bought Image as a present to her. Now she realized that wasn't the case.

Melanie set her glass back down on the table, spilling water on the linen cloth. Across the table Jazz sat quietly, his dark eyes studying her, as if trying to assess her reaction to the news.

Melanie knew it was unreasonable, but she didn't want to share Image with a spoiled rock star who only cared if she won high-stakes races. She wanted Image for her own.

Pushing back her seat, Melanie jumped up, mumbled something about needing some fresh air, and fled from the room. Will caught up with her halfway across the main dining area.

"Melanie, wait," he said, taking hold of her arm. "Jazz wasn't in on the deal until half an hour ago. I wanted to tell you before dinner, but you didn't get here in time. I know you're upset, but let me explain."

Melanie cut him off. "Of course I'm upset! How could you, Dad? How could you let Jazz in on it without even telling me?"

Uneasily Will glanced at the restaurant patrons, who were looking curiously at them. "Let's find someplace else to discuss this," he said in a low voice. Still holding her arm, he steered her from the dining room. When they reached the lobby, Melanie jerked her arm from his grasp. She strode out the front doors, the cold air slapping her in the face.

"Melanie, I had no choice," Will began.

Crossing her arms, Melanie turned away, unable to face him. Her whole body trembled from anger, not the cold.

"When I got back to the hotel, I called Susan and told her about buying Image," Will explained.

Susan. Melanie should have known. Melanie had always gotten along with her stepmother, but Susan was no horse person. She was, however, vice president of Graham Productions. When she found out what Will had done, she'd probably hit the roof.

"At first Susan couldn't believe I'd bought a racehorse, but when I explained the situation, she understood and even agreed with the idea. However, she quickly pointed out that Graham Productions didn't have five hundred thousand dollars in cash to invest. I started to panic, because I'd impulsively made a deal I couldn't honor. Jazz was listening to the conversation. He offered to go in on it with me."

Melanie turned. "And so you went right ahead without even mentioning it to me?"

"Well . . ." Will cleared his throat, suddenly uncomfortable. "When I hesitated, Jazz said that if I agreed, it would seal his contract with Graham Productions."

Melanie's jaw dropped.

"I couldn't say no, Melanie. Jazz and Pegasus are immensely talented. With the right management, they'll have a big career ahead of them. It would be an incredible opportunity for Graham Productions."

"You sold Image out for a record contract?"

"I'm a businessperson, and it was a business deal. Besides, Melanie, nothing has changed. You will still have complete responsibility for Image's training, and she'll remain at Whitebrook."

"But Jazz doesn't know anything about horse racing," Melanie insisted. "What happens when he gets sick of his latest toy? What happens when he decides to sell his half to the highest bidder—some stranger, or maybe even Brad Townsend?"

Just then Jazz came through the double doors. Melanie glared at him.

"Melanie," Will said, "I jumped at Jazz's offer because I didn't want to let you down."

"But don't you understand? You already have." Pushing past Will and Jazz, Melanie yanked open the door and rushed inside.

She'd already heard enough. Image was back where she'd started—an unpredictable horse with an unpredictable future.

"Mom and I need to talk to you, Melanie," Christina said, poking her head in the tack room door.

Melanie was sitting on a stool, the cheek piece of a bridle on her lap, a bucket of warm water by her feet. Bending, she sloshed a sponge in the water. It was Sunday morning. Earlier her father had left for New York and Jazz had left for Atlanta. Melanie had said a brief goodbye after dinner the night before, but she had been too hurt to face them in the morning. She'd decided to spend the morning cleaning tack to avoid talking to anyone. Obviously her strategy hadn't worked.

"I don't have anything to talk about," Melanie said, scrubbing the leather vigorously.

Ignoring her, Christina came in with Ashleigh right

behind her. They crossed the room and sat side by side on a tack trunk. Melanie grimaced. She really didn't feel like listening to a lecture.

"Your dad was devastated that you wouldn't speak to him this morning," her aunt began. "He hoped you would hear his side of the story."

"I heard it already," Melanie mumbled.

"Look, I realize you're angry because Will didn't buy Image for you as a gift," Ashleigh said. "But Melanie, you need to realize how unrealistic that is. This isn't Pony Club or 4-H. Thoroughbred racing is a business, and Image is an extremely valuable horse."

"I found that out the hard way. Look what happened when I wanted to buy Brad's half of Star," Christina chimed in. "There was no way Brad was going to sell him to me until Star became so sick that Brad thought he was worthless."

"We had a long talk at breakfast," Ashleigh continued. "I know you're upset that Jazz is going to own part of Image, too, but Will didn't have any choice, Melanie."

Melanie gave her a stubborn look, and Ashleigh went on.

"I don't know if your father mentioned that Brad actually threatened Fredericka. He said he'd go to the board of directors of the bank and demand that she pay her debts in full."

Melanie glanced up. "Brad could do that?"

Ashleigh nodded. "Brad is very powerful in this town. He's also a client of the same bank, and he can be extremely persuasive. After Image's fiasco yesterday, Fredericka had no choice but to sell. Your father had to make a instant decision or he would have lost Image to Brad."

Melanie realized how blind she had been. She'd been so excited about owning Image that she'd never once inquired about the details of the deal. Her father must have done some tricky finagling to get Image away from Brad so quickly.

"When Susan told your dad that Graham Productions wouldn't be able to swing it financially, Will panicked," Ashleigh went on. "The last thing he wanted to do was disappoint you. That's when Jazz made his offer."

"*Begged* is more like it," Christina said. "Jazz said he was afraid Will wouldn't take him seriously. And Will told us that Jazz was so excited, the whole way back to the hotel last night all Jazz talked about was Image . . . and *you*." Christina giggled. "What did you two talk about in the van, anyway?"

Melanie blushed. "Nothing."

"Anyway, Mel, please stop worrying about who owns Image," Ashleigh said firmly. "She's yours to train and race, and isn't that what you want?" Standing up, she came over to Melanie's stool. "And if our little lecture didn't convince you to quit moping, maybe this will." She held a racing program under Melanie's nose. "New Year's Eve, Turfway's hosting the Winter Debutante."

"And we think it will be the perfect race for Image," Christina exclaimed.

Melanie glanced at the program. She hadn't even thought about racing Image again, but the filly had a whole career ahead of her.

"The purse is higher, so it will attract a better grade of fillies," Ashleigh explained.

"We analyzed Image's race on Saturday," Christina added excitedly. "We decided that part of Image's problem was she got too far ahead of the others. We have to make sure that doesn't happen again. Mom called Vince, and even he agrees."

"Hmmm." Melanie furrowed her brow. "Image will be off probation by then. And it's three weeks away, which will give me enough time to work on her other problems. She's still a little funny at the gate." Tapping the brochure on her leg, she looked up at her aunt and cousin. "I've got some other ideas, too," she said. "Tell me what you think."

Ashleigh sat back down, and she and Christina listened intently.

"I'm going to force Image to work with lots of other horses. Every day this week I'll exercise her with a different set. Then, starting next weekend, I'll take her to Turfway and work her on their track. But no more leaving her there overnight. It's too stressful. On race day we'll van her over early in the morning. What do you think?"

"I think it's a great plan," Ashleigh agreed.

"Good." Setting the bridle down, Melanie stood up. "And thanks. You guys made me feel so much better. Now I've got to go talk to someone."

"Image?" Christina guessed.

"Nope. My dad," Melanie said as she opened the tack room door. "I owe him a really big apology."

On Saturday morning, December 31, the day of Turfway's Winter Debutante, Melanie unloaded Image from the Whitebrook van. The filly clattered down the ramp, then stood for a moment and smelled the crisp air. It had been three weeks since Image's disastrous race at Turfway, but since Melanie had vanned the filly to the track eight times in the past two weeks for morning works, Image was so used to the noise and confusion, she almost yawned.

"This is the big day," Melanie told her. "Your new owners are here to watch you, and they expect big things," she added, glancing around for her father and Jazz, who had arrived the night before.

Maybe Image wasn't nervous, but Melanie sure was. She had worked hard the last few weeks to prepare the filly for this day. She didn't want to disappoint Will and Jazz, but one mistake could be disastrous.

Melanie walked Image in front of Whitebrook's stalls to let her stretch and relax, and then she bent over to take off the filly's leg wraps.

"How's our horse?" Will asked, striding toward them in a sheepskin coat. "Is she ready?"

"She's ready," Melanie assured him, although she wasn't so sure herself.

"Jazz and I were checking out the odds, and the field looks pretty tough," Will continued, pacing in front of Image. "Tell me again why you picked this race."

"Because Image can handle it," Melanie replied.

"I guess you know that Brad Townsend's entered Flashy Miss. And he's got that Santiago guy riding her again."

Melanie's stomach tightened. She'd found out that morning that Brad had entered the filly, out of spite, no doubt.

"So, what's our strategy?" Will asked. "How are you going to keep Image from messing up?"

"I don't have a strategy," Melanie said and clenched her jaw. She wasn't sure this father-trainer relationship was going to work. Ever since Will and Jazz had arrived, they'd driven her crazy with their comments and questions.

"But Melanie, how are we going to win this thing without a plan?" Will demanded, frowning.

Pulling off the last wrap, Melanie straightened.

"Dad," she said in a low voice, "if you and Jazz don't like the way I'm training Image, then maybe you'd better hire a new trainer."

Will shook his head. "We don't want a new trainer. Jazz and I just want to stay informed. Remember, you've been doing this for a while. It's all new to us."

Melanie dropped her gaze. "Sorry. I'm just nervous, I guess."

"Don't be. You'll do great." Will reached out to hug her and then drew back. "Am I allowed to hug the trainer?" he joked.

Melanie wrapped her arms around him. "Only when she's your daughter and she needs one."

"Listen to this!" Jazz strode up in a ski parka and heavy boots, his eyes on the racing program. "Entries in the Winter Debutante: Tea for Two, two seconds in two starts. Sweetheart, breaks fast. Glory Be, won the Holiday Sweeps. Lollipop, a third and a second in two starts. Lucky Streak, one first, one second in three starts. And Angel Bay, ridden by Jorge Gonzales." Jazz glanced up. "Isn't he the jockey who won the Derby one year?"

"Your point?" Melanie fumed. "Other than trying to make me even more nervous than I already am?"

"Oh, sorry," Jazz apologized. "I just wanted to see what our game plan was. Especially since Flashy Miss is racing."

"Don't you two have anything better to do?"

Melanie asked. "Why don't you go spy on Brad or put a burr under Angel Bay's saddle pad?"

"Good idea." Will put his arm around Jazz and steered him away. "No more hovering."

Jazz stopped and turned toward Melanie. "If you let me stay here, I won't say a word. I promise."

Melanie relented. Will took the racing program and went off to find Ashleigh, Mike, and the others. Whitebrook wasn't racing any other horses, but a big group from the farm had come to watch Melanie and Image.

What if I let them down? Melanie thought as she led Image into her stall to groom her. Everyone had been so supportive, even when Image had been at her worst. Melanie knew that the best way to thank them was to win the race.

She hoped they could pull it off.

Melanie sighed and unbuckled Image's blanket.

"Can I help?" Jazz asked.

Sliding off the blanket, Melanie carried it over to the door. She'd spoken to her father several times since their argument, but this was the first time she'd talked to Jazz. He'd been off on a tour and hadn't flown in until late the night before.

"Sure." Melanie draped the blanket over the door and then pulled a brush from the grooming box and handed it to him. "She's ticklish by her right flank, so watch out."

They worked silently, Melanie on one side of

Image, Jazz on the other. Occasionally Melanie looked across Image's back to find Jazz watching her, but he didn't say anything.

Then Jazz began to hum a tune. A minute later Melanie joined him.

"That's a new song I'm writing," Jazz said.

"Catchy."

While Jazz brushed Image's tail, Melanie polished her hooves.

Finally Melanie couldn't stand it any longer. Straightening, she pointed the brush at Jazz. "So tell me the truth. Why did you want to buy Image in the first place?"

Jazz shrugged, as if the answer were obvious. "I like her. And I like being around the racetrack and the horses."

"Because it reminds you of the times you had with your father?"

"Yeah, but also because here, especially on the backside, I'm anonymous. No one cares who I am. I can breathe."

"But why Image? You could have had your pick."

"Why *not* Image?" Jazz countered.

Jazz came around to Melanie's side and stepped back to look at the filly. Melanie stepped back, too, and together they admired her. Image gleamed from head to toe. Her coat was like silk, and her muscles rippled. Turning her head, Image gazed at Melanie and Jazz, her expression curious, intelligent, and regal.

"You know why I chose Image?" Melanie asked softly. "Because of the look in her eyes."

Jazz nodded. "I know."

Melanie glanced up at him. "She wants to win, doesn't she?" she asked him, not caring if Jazz could really read horses' minds or not. She just needed reassurance. Any reassurance.

Jazz nodded. "That's what she's telling me."

"Then it's up to me, isn't it?" Melanie asked.

"Yes." Jazz looked down at her, a shadow of a smile on his lips. Melanie wasn't sure that was the reassurance she needed. But she was determined to do her best.

Melanie sighed. "Then I'd better not let her down."

"Last to load!" the starter announced.

Melanie tensed. The Winter Debutante was about to begin. In a few moments the starting bell would sound and all of Melanie's worries would dissolve in a rush of adrenaline.

Inhaling deeply, she looked over Image's ears and out the front of the narrow chute. For the past half hour a light snow had been falling, and the track stretched out before her like a frosted confection.

Because of the weather, Lollipop's owner had pulled her from the race. Two trainers had complained to the officials, trying to get it canceled. Sweetheart had almost flipped over in the post parade, spooked by the snow, and Glory Be had tried to run off.

But Image loved the snow. Ears pricked, she stared excitedly ahead, the flakes dusting her black mane with white. She snorted into the wind and danced on her toes.

"This is it," Melanie whispered, rubbing Image's withers.

The wind swirled snowflakes in the air, and the other fillies pranced and jigged in their chutes, delaying the starting bell. Image had drawn the number four position once more. Melanie hoped it wasn't their unlucky number. Flashy Miss, Sweetheart, and Glory Be were to her left. Angel Bay, Tea for Two, and Lucky Streak were on her right.

As they waited Image stood as if frozen, but Melanie could feel the horse's muscles quiver with anticipation. There were six furlongs between the starting gate and the finish line. Six furlongs to show the world what Image could do.

Then the starting bell rang and the front gates snapped open.

They were off!

Image blasted from the chute like an explosion, but Melanie had hold of her mane and stayed with the filly. The field had broken clean and even. She glanced left. Sweetheart, who had been in the number one chute, had leaped ahead to claim the rail; Flashy Miss and Glory Be were battling beside her. Melanie glanced right. Angel Bay, Tea for Two, and Lucky Streak galloped neck and neck, ahead of Image by a length. Mud and icy clumps flew from their hooves, hitting Melanie in the face. She dropped her goggles, then pulled on a second pair. But the snow clung to the lenses and she couldn't see.

Taking her reins in one hand, she pulled off the goggles and swiped at her eyes. The seven horses blew past the first quarter pole, and Melanie suddenly realized that Angel Bay and Lucky Streak were swerving in front of Image, trying to get closer to the rail. Their jockeys were riding aggressively, looking for every advantage.

Melanie gulped. This was not a field of hesitant fillies and inexperienced jockeys. The horses and riders weren't there to get experience; they were out to win.

Panicking, Melanie steered Image left and found herself behind Flashy Miss. Brushing the snow from her face, Melanie studied the field, hoping to find a hole. But Image was trapped behind a wall of churning hindquarters.

Don't panic, Melanie said to herself. *Think.*

Ducking her chin, she crouched low, avoiding the pelting mud. Eventually a hole would open. A horse would get tired, or someone would move ahead. Melanie had Image rated, and the filly still had lots more to give. Melanie told herself to be patient.

Then she saw her chance. Ricky Santiago was making his move for the rail. Beside Flashy Miss, Sweetheart was lagging. Glory Be was falling behind, too. A space was opening up. Melanie saw Ricky tug on the left rein, tilting Flashy Miss's head toward the rail. Gradually the filly swerved left to take the lead, leaving a narrow hole.

It was now or never.

"Go, Image," Melanie called, loud enough for the filly to hear above the pounding hooves. Image's ears flicked back and her stride lengthened. But Jorge, Angel Bay's jockey, had seen the same hole.

"No!" Melanie hollered as Jorge snatched Angel Bay's head to the left and drove the filly into the gap, bumping Image out of the way.

Melanie wanted to scream with frustration, but she had no time. There were only two furlongs left.

Her only chance was to swing wide around the whole field. It would take tremendous effort, but Melanie had no choice. If ever she needed to have faith in Image's speed and heart, it was now.

Tugging on the right rein, Melanie signaled Image to veer to the outside. The filly hesitated momentarily, as if confused, then obeyed. Slowly they pulled up beside Tea for Two, the outside horse. Icy mud pelted them like hailstones. Melanie frowned, worried that the filly would give up under the mud and the effort.

Then Image shook her head angrily, and Melanie felt her rhythm change, as if she were shifting gears.

Stretching out her neck, Image lengthened her stride and blew past Tea for Two and Lucky Streak as though they were standing still.

Melanie wanted to laugh, but her lips were wet and frozen. Her fingers were numb on the reins, and snow was stuck to her eyelashes. She glanced to her left. Sweetheart and Glory Be were straggling. Flashy Miss and Angel Bay were fighting for the lead. Neither of their jockeys had even noticed Image.

"Let's do it," Melanie whispered. She hunkered low and let Image go. With immense strides the filly galloped straight for the finish line, leaving the others far, far behind. Melanie was bursting inside, but she kept a firm grip on the reins and a level head. This time there would be no mistakes.

They roared past the grandstand and the cheering crowd, four lengths ahead of Flashy Miss and Angel Bay, the gap widening with each stride. The finish line was only a few feet away.

Melanie could hold back the happiness no longer. A smile cracked her frozen cheeks. Elation bubbled inside her.

This was what she'd been working toward all these months.

This was what she'd been dreaming about all her life.

Racing Image.

ALICE LEONHARDT has been horse-crazy since she was five years old. Her first pony was a pinto named Ted. When she got older, she joined Pony Club and rode in shows and rallies. Now she just rides her quarter horse, April, for fun. The author of more than thirty books for children, she still finds time to take care of two horses, two cats, two dogs, and two children, as well as teach at a community college.